Faith Richmond came to Australia from New Zealand when she was very young. The third of four children, she spent most of her childhood years in Brisbane, Canberra and later Melbourne, and her memories of the Canberra of the 1940s evoke perhaps the most poignant of her experiences in the book.

While *Remembrance* is her first book, the author has won several awards for writing, including a prize in the Australian Society of Women Writers' competition. Her interest in literature is varied, from Jung and existentialism to poetry, and she has a special interest in the detailed observation that all forms of art require. She paints and draws, and her illustrations were the first to be used on Melbourne TV in 1956. Until taking up writing, she illustrated books for publication.

IMPRINT

REMEMBRANCE

FAITH RICHMOND

COLLINS PUBLISHERS
AUSTRALIA

IMPRINT

COLLINS PUBLISHERS AUSTRALIA

First Published in 1988 by William Collins Pty Ltd,
55 Clarence Street, Sydney NSW 2000

Reprinted 1989

Copyright © Faith Richmond, 1988

National Library of Australia
Cataloguing-in-Publication data:

Richmond, Faith.
Remembrance : a daughter's story.
ISBN 0 7322 2420 9.
1. Richmond, Faith – Childhood and youth. 2. Fathers
and daughters – Australia – Biography. I. Title.
920.72'0994

All rights reserved. No part of this publication may be reproduced,
stored in a retrieval system, or transmitted, in any form, or
by any means, electronic, mechanical, photocopying, recording or
otherwise, without the prior permission of the publishers.

This book is sold subject to the condition that it shall not,
by way of trade or otherwise, be lent, resold, hired out or
otherwise circulated without the publisher's prior consent
in a form of binding or cover other than that in which it is
published and without a similar condition including this condition
being imposed on the subsequent purchaser.

Typeset in 10/12pt Times Roman by Love Computer Typesetting, Sydney
Printed by Globe Press, Victoria

Cover illustration: *Flowerpiece on a Table* by Grace Cossington-Smith

In memory of Jenny Hedding (née Peverill)
who died from leukaemia on 2 May 1987.

'There's rosemary, that's for remembrance. Pray you, love, remember. And there is pansies, that's for thoughts . . . There's rue for you, and here's some for me. We may call it herb of grace o'Sundays. O, you must wear your rue with a difference. There's a daisy. I would give you some violets, but they withered all when my father died.'

Ophelia

Acknowledgements

I owe much gratitude to Charles Edward Leopold (Ted) who, during the writing of this book gave so freely his time, his patience and his garden to write in. Very special thanks must go also to John Pinkney for his most valuable advice on construction and syntax and for his gentle curbing of my literary excesses.

And to those who helped and encouraged me: my children, my siblings, Edith and Ted Wall, Kris Hemensley, the women at the Whitehorse Centre, Margot Escott, Rosemary Nissen, Philip Martin, Kristin Henry and all the other members of the Poets' Union, Carmel Hart, Paddy Duane for his help with scientific and technical advice, and Carole Smith and Robin Pinkney who so willingly took on the typing marathon on completion of the manuscript ... and to so many others who listened as *Remembrance* progressed – thank you.

The publishers would like to thank Mrs J.S. Mills for permission to reproduce the cover picture, *Flowerpiece on a Table* by Grace Cossington-Smith.

Some of the characters in this book are real, some are imaginary and others are composites.

1
GOD AND MISS HAZELWOOD

I stand in front of the easel and dip the long thick brush into the jar of sunny yellow. I put the tip of the bristles on my tongue. The paint tastes of nothing. Then I start my father's face. I draw a beautiful round shape that when I've finished has no beginning and no end. I put the brush back and take another colour. This time I do the hair. It curves over the head and hangs down.

I think of my parents in our house next door. My mother in the garden. My father probably sitting by his study window writing. I'll paint him as I imagine him with his hair falling across his forehead; and some strands on the side reaching almost to his cheek. The eyes are next in a different colour. I do the mouth then his orange trousers. Miss Hazelwood stands beside me:

'That's a nice picture but what a funny colour for the gentleman's trousers. And what long hair you've given him. Men have short hair.'

'It's not a gentleman. It's daddy.'

'But daddies wear trousers in *this* colour.'

She takes another brush from its jar and covers the lovely orange with thick wet black. And coats my father's favourite trousers with the black paint:

'There! That's better!'

She unclips the sheet and takes it away:

'It'll be dry by the time your mother collects you.'

We sit on a square of flowered carpet:

'Cross your legs children to make room for everyone and button up your lips. Before today's song I'd like to say a very special prayer. It's for all the young men who will be going away to the war. And for the poor children in Poland who are suffering so much under the Nazis.'

My parents talk a lot about the Nazis so I know who they are. They kill people who've done nothing wrong. I look behind Miss Hazelwood as she sits on one of our little lunchtime chairs. There's the picture of Mary with baby Jesus. And above the dolls' corner beyond, hangs a portrait of the King. But the one I like best is near the blocks. It hangs in a dark wooden frame. It shows a little girl in a frilled pinafore, holding a long slender stick as she walks behind her line of geese. The birds' white cheeks are rounded and give a sweet expression to their faces. Some of them have open beaks. They waddle beside a row of dark flat-looking trees at the roadside. Voluptuous clouds above, puff and bundle along, sharing the sky with a round sun whose rays are lines that dip into the topmost leaves. Miss Hazelwood starts the song. As she sings, the little gold cross round her neck captures the light for a moment and the chain which holds it moves against her throat, its links shining too:

> *'There is a happy land far, far away*
> *Where Saints in glory stand all through the day.'*

Oh! I've heard that one! My mother sings it, so I join in. Miss Hazelwood stops suddenly and looks at us:
    'Who was that? Which of you knows that song?'
    I feel very important:
    'My mummy sings that at home.'
    'Would you like to stand up for us all?'
    Miss Hazelwood smiles at me. It's hard to get up as the other children are pressed so close. I love singing but I feel the eyes of the others on me as I stand so tall among them. I hold my blue dress in tight fists at my sides:

> *'There is a boarding house far, far away*
> *Where tripe and onions cook all through the day,*
> *Oh how the boarders yell . . .'*

Miss Hazelwood's face has changed. She shakes her head. My

stomach turns over and I tighten my grip on my dress. She looks toward me, frowning:

'I think we'll have to send you to the office. Those are not the correct words at all.'

I stumble through the children who sit staring up at me. My eyes prickle with tears. I can hardly see where I'm going. I wait in the office. Grown-ups are always angry and you never know why. I hear Miss Hazelwood talking gently to the children. She mentions my name. Then she starts singing the song again. I look around the room. It's dark in here with the blind half drawn. I haven't got a hanky so I wipe my eyes and nose on my dress. Then I cross to the window and put my chin on the sill. I can see Angela Clark's house across the road. David Clark's nappies flap on the verandah rail. There's Peter Clark's wooden billycart in the front garden. And the family's singing bird in its cage on the porch. A dog trots by below the window not far from where I stand. The man who sharpens people's knives goes past in his cart. The horse's face is almost obscured by a nosebag of chaff. His owner has cut holes in a wide-brimmed hat which the horse wears, its ears black peeping triangles. I can just hear through the closed window the jingle of the harness and the man's rough voice as he lifts a long stick in the air and flicks it on the horse's back. Something in the sky distracts me. I look up and see a thick flock of blackbirds wheel across the roof of the Clarks'. As the birds change direction together they look, just for a moment, like short dark pencil strokes. Then they're black dots again and grow small as a sprinkling of pepper as they disappear past distant chimney pots. There's a burst of noise as the children in the big room next door go outside to play. I turn as Miss Hazelwood enters. She sits down behind the desk:

'The words you sang were not very nice.'

'Mummy sings it like that.'

I want to go to the toilet. I put my hand between my legs to hold it in.

'When we're singing about God we must use nice words.'

'Mummy and daddy don't believe about God so I don't.

They said it's an animal.'

I search my memory for the right word:

'A panther.'

Miss Hazelwood looks sharply at me.

'I see.'

She clasps and unclasps her hands on the desk:

'Is your mother at home now?'

'Oh yes because our baby's asleep.'

'She lets you walk home by yourself sometimes doesn't she?'

I smile at her:

'Yes, because I'm four and a half now.'

'Well I'm afraid I'll have to ask you to go home. You may not return. I'll speak to your parents this afternoon when nursery school is finished. Don't forget your hat. You may also take your painting.'

As I walk through the playground I remember the conversation last week about God. My mother and father sat in the sitting room after dinner. My sister, who's nearly six, was reading a little book her friend had lent her. She looked up at my parents:

'Why do they keep saying "God" in this story. What is God?'

My parents had laughed together and looked at each other. My mother spoke first:

'People don't know how to explain the world properly so they say that a being called God made it for us in six days.'

My sister looked astonished:

'You mean, made it *all* in six days?'

'Yes, that's why it's so silly. I can't believe that, so I don't believe in God.'

My sister had started reading again. But I saw my father smile a lot and lean toward my mother. I remember he wore his orange trousers.

'What do you say,' he said, as he touched her arm, 'perhaps we should tell her that God is a pantheist!'

I'm sitting in my usual place at the dining-room table. My father is at one end with the front half of the *Courier Mail* and my mother is sitting on my left at this end with the back half. My sister is opposite me and watches closely everything I do. My big brother has finished breakfast and is outside making something out of wood. My blue-eyed baby brother bangs the cream-painted tray of his high-chair with a rusk.

When I move my head slightly to the left and look through the crimson part of the window, the jacaranda flowers in the back garden turn purple just in that spot and when I resume my position they go back to being blue. Sometimes I change places with my big brother and see pink chooks darting around in their run, down at the back of the long garden. My mother has gone to the dark kitchen which is next to this room and I get down from my chair, being careful not to sweep *The French Revolution*, which gives me extra height, to the floor. She's standing at the stove waiting for the eggs to boil. I hitch myself onto the kitchen table nearby and watch tiny linked bubbles streaming from three of the eggs. I lean across and put my arms around her long calico apron to butt her skinny stomach with my head. But she's too preoccupied to respond.

I can hear my father saying something softly in the next room. His paper rustles as he turns the page. We have cold sausages which my father has cut up small for me but when I blur my eyes they suddenly look like cockroaches, so I secrete them slowly and carefully into the pockets of my calico nightie while my mother is busy reading. Anyway I don't like meat much. I go to the butcher's with my mother. There are white lambs painted on the tiled walls. They gambol in green grass with pretty daisies growing and clouds above. And in the trays below are parts of their bodies. Rows of little dead pink commas that you're supposed to eat. I always shuffle in the butcher's sawdust till it's untidy and you can see the wooden floor. He shouldn't be happy. He should be sad for the lambs that can't run any more.

My father, in response to a question from my mother, leaves the table and, with his toast knife, points to a map of the world that he has on the wall near the bathroom door. My mother looks sad:

'So that's France and Poland. Oh dear.'

I tune in at times to my parents' conversation but mostly I watch my baby brother in his high-chair. I plan to do a drawing of him tomorrow. My aunt has sent from Sydney some pastels that you draw with, then wet with a brush so it looks like paint. My brother's eyes dart across the room and back as he follows a jackadandy. The cats sit on the windowsill where they catch the slight morning breeze that no one else notices. With small jerks of their heads, they too follow the darting light. It forms a concentrated quivering square almost still for a moment. Then it suddenly elongates to a blur bending at the ceiling. I look across to my father and for some reason my heart wrenches. His throat and under his chin shine softly yellow like honey on white bread as the gold cigarette case lends its colour to his skin. Then the lid snaps shut and the cats' eyes widen momentarily as the match flares and my father draws on his cigarette.

The baby chews his now-limp rusk and drains his boat-shaped bottle. I watch him long and hard, hating and loving him and wondering if he knows that I'm not hungry or thirsty and that we are separate children. My sister asks my mother a question about growing and, as they speak together, I understand something I've been wondering about. Until this moment I've always thought that the reason our dresses get shorter is that the hems are eaten slowly in the nights by moths in the wardrobes. There's a still moment while I absorb the startling new truth I've just heard. I'm aware, in this time of revelation, that both my hands clasp the bowl hard in front of me. I look at the rabbits running round its rim then through the window at my brother who's down near the chook run with the new wooden glider he's made. I understand what my mother and sister are saying, but with difficulty and a sense of sadness. So you grow *all* the time. But so does everyone else. The hems have nothing to do with the moths. My brother's nearly nine and I'd always thought that one day we'd be the same age. That we'd be able to play together as big children do in the street. I won't ever catch up.

He'll stop when he's a grown-up and so will I – but later than him. The man up in Bowen Street must have grown until he was much older. He towers over the tallest of people.

I turn to my mother and ask her what 'wretched' means – she called me that one hot day recently while we were on the verandah. She was sewing and I was breathing in the scent of her rose garden and listening to the deafening trill of the grasshoppers. Before she answers, she puts her finger on the word she is up to and glances at me, distracted:

'It means unfortunate.'

I turn back to bury my face in my glass of milk. I'm so disappointed. I'd hoped it might mean 'beautiful'. The covers of the *Revolution* shift slightly as I put my empty glass back on the table. I look at the creamed honey. It has an 'h' and another letter I recognise from my name – I think it's 't'. I turn to my father:

'What does that *little* writing say?'

He pauses in his reading:

'Twice as nice if kept on ice.'

The blue and white linen curtains bulge softly into the room as the Brisbane westerly gains strength. My mother found the material in an obscure basement shop in town and had just enough coupons to buy the last of the bolt. She found that there wasn't quite enough so she joined some old sheeting onto the bottom. Where the join showed she embroidered a line of turquoise peacocks. It's odd how you can't remember your numbers at nursery school but you know you'll always think of those peacocks. My father is buttering more toast for my baby brother. He still has a Tally Ho cigarette paper hanging by its corner from his bottom lip. My sister catches my eye and we look away quickly before we smile. Our father makes us laugh so much but we never tell him why. He smears Vegemite on the baby's toast in tiny little dib-dabs, very daintily with his huge hand. I daren't look anywhere near my sister. At other times he plays the piano. He loves the music so much that his head jerks from side to side at particular moments and tears run down his cheeks and neck. My sister and I ache to hug him, but instead we stuff our mouths with cushions to stop laughing. My mother says my father is sentimental.

I dip my finger in the dish of marmalade then suck it just so that I can have the excruciating taste of the sip of milk that follows. Milk after bacon tastes sweet as honey but milk after marmalade is bitter as my mother's quinine. It interests me that it's not the milk's fault that it tastes so horrible. My mother says it's bath time and disappears through the adjoining door. She lights the Caliphont. It booms and roars. Water gushes into the lion-legged bath. My sister goes first and after ten minutes I step into cool, soapy, greenish water. I can sit as long as I like today. I've been suspended from nursery school because of the song. My mother talked to Miss Hazelwood and I'm allowed back in two weeks.

When I lie with my head under water, the wind, the grasshoppers, my mother's loud voice and the baby's crying, all disappear suddenly and completely. I can make deafening noises by moving the metal soap dish along the bottom of the tub. My knees though, little dry ovals like islands, must never be submerged or I'll have bad luck for the rest of my life – my sister told me that. When I surface I can hear the familiar stop-start cacophony of my mother's treadle machine. I step from the bath onto the wooden lattice mat, dry, and dress myself, remember to wet my toothbrush, and turn back to pull out the plug. The baby's screams remind me that he hates the noise. I feel a mixture of apprehension, sorrow and pleasure. My mother is comforting him and I wait to be punished for forgetting. I look at her face and I'm not sure how I feel.

She has a round garden bed on the nature strip – she calls it the frontage. It glows with sunset-pink geraniums and phlox and gerberas. When she's kneeling weeding this bed with her feet tucked under her bottom, the sight of her soles in a little vee makes me feel like crying with love – and sadness too, I think mostly sadness. My mother's famous in our suburb for many reasons:

The circular garden bed that the whole street shares with her.

Her refrigerator with its finned cylinder on top and enamelled cabriole legs.

The egg beater my father bought her. It has a metal disc which fits snugly over a specially made basin.

Because she hoses the kids with suits and slicked hair as they pass by on Sunday to the Temperance League. She aims as accurately as she can for their Bibles.

And of course for the trousers she wears. Sometimes when she brings my forgotten lunch into the playroom at nursery school, I wish she was wearing a pleated skirt like the other mothers.

My sister pushes her chair back:

'Come on, we'll play dollsies on the verandah till I have to go to school.'

We take our new cutout books into the sun. They're called The Little Princesses. My sister's is Princess Elizabeth and mine is Princess Margaret Rose. There are cardboard pages of the girls in underwear. They have dots around them and you press them out and bend back the tabs so they can stand. On thinner leaves we cut out tab-shouldered dresses for occasions such as garden parties and walks with nurse. There are nighties trimmed with a profusion of broderie anglaise and threaded with royal blue satin ribbons, and small black shoes with straps and buttons. I wish my mother would make me clothes like these. But when I ask she always says:

'Frills and furbelows are common.'

I might think that too when I'm grown up. But I don't now.

My mother loves cemeteries. We're going for a steam-train ride to see one today, far away from Auchenflower. I sit on my mother's lap so that I can see through the window. My baby brother screams whenever we go through black tunnels. Sometimes the train driver remembers to put on the carriage lights but I suppose he doesn't always think it necessary. I can smell the dust on the window ledge. And someone's left a half-sucked Butter Menthol in one of the corners. I'd like to put it in my mouth when we speed through one of the dark passages under the hills. I can imagine my fingers quickly prising it free – and the sweet hot taste of it on my tongue. But I think of the trouble there'll be if my mother smells it on my breath. So I leave it. But its inviting golden presence stays with me and I look at it as much as I do the scenery. Before and after the tunnels there are steep banks and cuttings. They're smothered with blue rockface plants and green creepers and seem to be only inches from the train's window.

Christmas is coming soon. It's the first time I've known beforehand. Last year I seemed to have no warning – suddenly it was Christmas Day and I was unwrapping a wooden duck on the end of a long stick. When you pushed it, the bird's painted wings would flap up and down. My baby brother plays with it now, when I let him – but the colours aren't bright anymore. I got a mouth-organ too and played it for hours until my lips were numb and tasted of tin and my head was reeling. In the train to the cemetery my father starts singing:

> *'Ding dong merrily on high,*
> *In Heav'n the bells are ringing,*
> *Ding dong verily the sky,*
> *Is riv'n with angels' singing.'*

He demonstrates the harmony for the Gloria part at the end and my sister copies him. They sing together. And laugh a lot. Then they practise some more and try again. And it sounds like the radio. The baby even stops crying to listen.

We arrive at the station and walk to the cemetery. My mother dashes from one headstone to another. She clambers laughing, onto oblongs of marble. And over the fancy little iron fences. She leans across to part dried grasses and to peer at gold-leaf names and dates. At one of them she stops to say to my father:

'Oh dear, look at this one – 1917, killed in action . . . so young . . . and now it's all starting again.'

She shakes her head and moves on. The baby sits on a path in his yellow, bloomered sunsuit patting the earth beside him and looking with interest at his dirty little palms. My mother strolls between the rows then stops to read out the inscriptions on two adjacent white headstones that rise at right-angles from short flower-covered mounds:

'HENRY WILLIAM WHITE
FEBRUARY 1892 – NOVEMBER 1892
AGED NINE MONTHS.
DIED IN A FALL FROM HIS PERAMBULATOR.'

She looks then at the grave alongside:
'Oh Norman, what a terrible thing! They were twins! Listen:

EMILY IRIS WHITE
FEBRUARY 1892 – MARCH 1893
AGED THIRTEEN MONTHS
DIED OF MELANCHOLY.'

My mother rises from her kneeling position and dusts the earth and prickles from the thick stockings she wears. She doesn't look at any more graves but sits alone on a stone nearby and stares across the white-dotted landscape of the cemetery. I leave to join my father and sister further on. As I walk down the path toward them I wonder, with a sudden shock, if Miss Preston will be lying here soon. We went to see her last week. My mother said she'd had a stroke. At first that description of her illness sounded soft like caressing a cat. But when my sister said, 'With one stroke of his sword the enemy's head fell to the ground', it suddenly had frightening overtones. When we visited her, my mother had pushed me forward and I'd leaned on tip-toe to kiss the old lady's cheek. Her skin was fine like rice paper and felt soft as suede, but I drew back hastily in case death could be catching. We'd had apple cake brought in by her sister. It was warm from the oven. The steaming fruit was translucent and palest green with flecks of nutmeg like babies' freckles. The old lady left most of hers. The thought of her lying here whitely – under the ground – is almost unimaginable. Poor Miss Preston.

I reach my father, who strolls with the baby on his hip. He turns as I catch up and nips my cheek with his thumb and forefinger:

'And here's little skinnymalinks – with us at last, after her snail's-pace journey. What's mummy doing up there still?'

'I s'pose she's thinking of the two dead babies.'

My father puts one flat hand above his eyes like the brim of a hat and stares back for a full minute at my mother who's still sitting on the stone. He seems indecisive, hesitates and starts to say something. Then turns back to continue his downward walk past the headstones and straggling grass on the dirt track through the cemetery. I watch him from behind. Thank goodness he'll never die. My mother says he's needed at the university. He won't be going to the war.

Some of the fathers went last year. One of them who lives up in Kellett Street has come back with bad injuries. The ship he was on was bombed. He's the father of one of the 'littlies' that have an afternoon sleep at Nursery School. My sister and I pass their house on the way to the milk shop. We know we shouldn't stare, but we can't help looking a bit. He sits in a wicker chair in his garden near the front gate with a checked rug over his lap. Although his eyes hold blank mysteries, sometimes they move with us as we pass on the other side of the street. He has a look of empty sadness. Part of him came home from the war. The rest has yet to return.

I've thought a lot about illness and death since our visit to Miss Preston and the cemetery. The Murphys' house up in Pennington Street burned to a fragile shell last Tuesday. The fire engines roared up Munro Street past our house and my baby brother woke screaming from his afternoon nap. Ever since, I've been riding my tricycle up there. I see the hills of Auchenflower between the sticky, black blistered window-frames where the walls used to be. There are pieces of buckled iron and grotesque springs. I think I smell death in my nostrils. I sniff the bubbled remains of doors that once opened onto scenes of cheerful, unsuspecting ordinariness. And I can't help staring at the blackened iron cot in the garden where Valda Murphy's brother died. I suppose he'll be in the cemetery now like the little twins. On Saturday, after lunch, a woman walks toward me, apronned and with silver clips in her hair. She stands in the stubby charred grass of the Murphys' garden, hands on hips and leaning forward:

'You come straight out of there *this minute*! Those walls could collapse any time. Your mummy would *slay* you if she knew you were here!'

I take my tricycle and ride slowly home.

2
THE LONG DAYS

It's February the fourth – my first day of school. I can't hear my mother. It must be very early. I lie for some time looking at the faces I can see in the plaster rose around the light. The doves in the big trees beyond the verandah are stirring and starting their day. I listen to their voices:

'It's about time, too.'

'It's about time, too.'

Then one that's different:

'It's not true. It's not true.'

I lean on one elbow and look out at a morning that seems freshly outlined and strangely still. Across the dim nursery in his cot, my baby brother humps asleep with a flushed cheek. If I get my drawing things so early he might wake and bring my mother in, cross and whispering from the kitchen. My mother always wakes soon after five and is sipping tea, so she tells me, at half past. She reads either Karl Marx, her Communist magazines, or the latest Graham Greene. I think she remembers then the red-haired soldier she was going to marry who was killed in India. Sometimes I'd like to share the mysteries of her solitary dawn but I'd feel like an intruder if I tiptoed in. By six she's drunk her tea and cut and wrapped our lunches (four of them now, I tell myself).

One morning while Breakfast Delite formed craters in the pot and the ice man clattered up next door's drive, she told me that she chooses the soft waxed sort of lunch paper from the grocer so she won't wake us while packing the sandwiches. I looked up at her brown face then and I learned, in that moment, many things. The baby stirs and whimpers and with a sigh is asleep again. The lightshade in our nursery is fawn and fly-spotted and tilted with string toward my bed. I can draw and look at books at night while my brother grizzles, plays with his toes and finally settles. I listen now to next door's lawnmower, often indistinguishable from my father's snoring in the next room and sometimes miraculously in time with it. My stomach tightens as I remember today. I think about the schoolhouse opposite where I'll have to sit at a desk, like my sister, and there'll be no toys.

Last month the infant school and kindergarten with their little second storey Church burned to the ground. Today and for some time, I will be going to temporary premises which consist of a disused timber house opposite ours – high up beyond a steep curving driveway. At breakfast my mother seems kinder and talks to me more than usual, and my father makes a joke about how quiet the house will be. I hug my dolls and try to swallow my toast which my father has specially cut into fingers. Though I feel some excitement when I touch my new cardboard case, I would happily swap the starched dress and stiff new school shoes for my sister's usual hand-me-downs and her old sandals that pinch. At eight-thirty I kiss my baby brother seventeen times on his plump surprised cheek and my father takes my face between his hands and all I can see are his blue eyes blurred and distorted by my tears. His fingers are warm and dry and they smell of tobacco. My mother takes my hand and we cross the road together while my father stands inside our gate with the baby on his shoulders and calls:

'Good luck for the great adventure!'

At school children play on swings that sound like magpies calling. Some, established already in small groups, swap cards and marbles while others stand bridging the time between home and school, reluctant and tentative. I eat my lunch at playtime and a teacher chastises me for my stupidity. At twelve o'clock the others have banana sandwiches and drink raspberry cordial from narrow-necked glass bottles. Their sandwiches are wrapped in damp tea-towels. I watch Billy Rudd spill his milk down his grey jumper as he hiccups back sobs that he's been holding in all the morning. Milk runs down over his voluminous shorts and sad little frightened legs and mixes with his urine before trickling off diluted down the path. Even my new lunch box fails to cheer me, and the small wrapped sweet my mother has put in it for the first day reminds me too much of home. The day is so long. I watch the big kids. My sister is among them and totally ignores me. They do the strangest things. A row of them makes an archway and others in a line go through. The big kids are singing:

> *'Oranges and lemons,*
> *The bells of St Clemens,*
> *You owe me three farthings,*
> *When will you pay me,*
> *Today or tomorrow?'*

Other children stand around picking the surface of the wool off each other's cardigans. They tug and pull and when they have a large palm-full of fuzz they put it in their pockets and go on to someone else with a different colour. Then suddenly something dreadful happens. A girl with short black hair lies in the sandpit. She's twitching all over. Her legs are moving back and forth – her heels rubbing in the sand. They leave two bald tracks. I feel sick as I watch her. Yet I can't stop looking. I find I've sat down on the ground with a hard thud. Then two of the teachers run quickly to the girl in the sandpit and one of them calls over her shoulder:

'It's Dulcie – get the peg – quick!'

They crouch around her. They're doing something to her face but I can't see what. After a minute or two her legs stop moving. The teachers disperse and the black-haired girl, who I'll be frightened of forever, digs in the sand and talks to her friend as if nothing had happened.

After lunch we choose shiny coloured paper shapes from a box and glue them onto sheets of paper. You can really only make houses and roofs and boat sails. I'd like to draw my mother and a garden of flowers around my red house with its yellow triangular roof, but I don't know if you're permitted to ask for a pencil. Then our teacher, Miss O'Shea, teaches us a song. It's about a man who goes around dropping grains of sand on your eyes to make you shut them at bedtime.

> *The sandman grey, steals on his way,*
> *Scattering your eyelids with sand.*

We have to sing it over and over. Miss O'Shea walks along in front of our desks, hands raised to demonstrate the sandman. Her fingers twinkle in the air. I'm glad I share the nursery with my brother. I don't think it's true about the sandman but I'm going to make sure I stay awake tonight so I'll be certain. Suddenly all the kids are scraping back their chairs and running to the door. We are allowed to play on the swings and seesaws for ten minutes.

I need to be by myself. I cross the path and step over the grass. There are some bushes next to the fence. I stand behind them and at last I feel safe. No one can see me. I walk down to the gate at the bottom of the steep drive to look across at our house. There's my father! I want to call out. I want him to rescue me and put me on his shoulders as he sometimes does, then run down the middle of the road roaring, till the neighbours twitch at their curtains to look out. But he only does that on special days. He would be too busy today – I see that he's painting the verandah posts yellow as egg yolk and I can hear him singing even from here. The other fathers never do the things mine does when he's feeling happy. Sometimes I feel sorry for other children . . .

I run my fingertips along the school fence . . . bp- bp- bp- bp- bp- bp. Soon my hand is so numb I have to look down to see that it's still attached to my arm. I look across at my father then return to the other children. This day is going on forever. Inside we each have a box of shells. You have to put them in rows of two then three then four. The shells are cold to touch. Most of them have delicate little spirals and a minaret-sharp tip. But two of mine are small white fan shapes with ridges. I turn them over and see that the inside is palest mushroom pink and glossy. Miss O'Shea passes down the aisle between our desks and stops at mine. She takes the pink shell from my hands and places it firmly in its box:

'Do your fours now – this isn't playtime, you know.'

I arrange them in their neat rows.

I wonder what my mother's doing now. I bet she's hugging my baby brother or talking sweetly to him as she buckles his shoes for a walk. I hear a strange scratching noise. When I look up I see that Miss O'Shea has drawn shapes on the blackboard. She taps with a stick on the wooden surround till all the children's heads are up and watching:

'Now we'll do pothooks – my assistant will give you an exercise book and pencil.'

I long for my dolls, my drawing book and pastels and my baby brother even though he pulls my hair. And I could cry for the scent of my mother's cheek and the biscuity smell of her apron.

3
PARENTS AND SIBLINGS

My father is thirty-nine years old. His hair was fair but is mostly grey now. He has little puffs of flesh above and below each eye and these make his face look vulnerable. And he has a long nose and chin. Every few weeks my mother sits him on a wooden kitchen chair under the blue jacaranda. She tucks a tea-towel in his shirt collar and trims his hair. The neighbour's radio plays through the open Sunday window:

> *'It don't make sense to chicka, chicka,*
> *boom chick.'*

A striped cat sits on our fence to watch. My father is always reading even while she snips. He holds his book out in front of him with long straight arms and there's trouble from my mother when he has to turn a page. The haircut over, she flicks the tea-towel. Once I saw my father's hair caught amid lantana bushes. Some of it had blown onto the road. I stood looking at it and thinking that a part of my father had blown away forever.

He makes things that other people would probably like to have, but don't think of. He put a nail in my mother's wooden dish-mop handle so that it can perch on the edge of the sink. It used to enrage her by falling under the hot suds all the time. He built her a three-sided screen made with a timber frame and covered with layers of hessian, so she can sit among the bees in the garden. She can read and shelter from the wind by turning it in any direction she likes. In winter she can catch the sun as she endlessly knits jumpers. When it's cool she looks for where the cats have found warmth and situates her screen there beside them.

Sometimes to give my mother a rest my father takes us all to the Regent in town. He strides through the city streets with my little brother sitting high on his shoulders. I run along behind and my sister takes enormous steps to keep level with him so she can talk. When we cross the intersections he takes my hand and squeezes it hard to make me laugh in agony when my bones crackle. He buys a huge bag of lamingtons and Richmond Maids of Honour and offers them so often during the film that sometimes we have two in our hands at once. My sister and I never tell him that our mother buys one block of chocolate at the pictures and that you're meant to wait ten minutes between squares. He buys the week's vegetables on the way home at the Dinkum Aussie Fruit Shop in Roma Street. When my father is marking exam papers we aren't allowed to play on the verandah outside his window. Or anywhere in the garden on the study-side of the house. But once when our mother is out, we dash across the lawn naked, scaling the profusion of deck chairs, toys and flower beds. Our father thunders out from his study shouting:

'Bloody children!'

When he catches us his smack is so light and tentative we can barely feel it. He retreats satisfied and we rush to the sitting room and bury our faces in the sofa to muffle our uncontrollable laughter.

Every few days my mother dry-mops our varnished timber floors. Dust swirls around our nostrils and hovers in the broad bands of Brisbane sunlight that slope into the rooms. My father stands in the doorway sometimes and says rather sadly:

'My mother always found an O'Cedar mop was best.'

When our parents go letter-boxing to distribute pamphlets, people throw things at them from windows and doorways and chase them down front paths yelling: 'Get back to Russia where you belong!'

My mother laughs and calls back something clever and sarcastic but my father flinches and walks quickly away.

My parents don't quarrel. Well, not in front of us. My mother goes her own way and my father is too gentle to criticise. But sometimes he reminds me of the Charlie Chaplin film we saw. He puts on brightly coloured clothes – once he wore my sister's yellow tutu from ballet – and strides around making loud speeches. It seems to be at special times that he does these funny things. And it's not very often. I asked my mother on one occasion if it was his birthday that made him so happy and she looked angry and said his birthday was six months away. When I was five and a half, he came into the nursery early in the morning and read aloud. With his hand spread out, he looked like someone on a stage. Then my mother appeared and pushed him out, closing the door. I heard him say:

'Don't you want me to enjoy myself?'

There are many beautiful things about my mother. She is thirty-seven and her face is smooth. It has no shadows of time yet. She laughs a lot and when she smiles her cheeks show soft dimples. Her hair is as dark and shiny as Black Beauty's mane. Her eyes are as brown as a squirrel's and she has black, often angry, eyebrows. Sometimes we ask if we are adopted like our older brother, because not one of the three of us has brown eyes. My mother's skin is sand-coloured from gardening under the Queensland sun.

While oxtail stew fills the room with its fragrance in the late afternoons, she plays the piano and sings. She has some favourites from the *Oxford Song Book* and her voice, although light and quivery, keeps well in tune. It's strange that her normal talking voice is so loud that it's almost a shout. Yet her singing is soft and you feel at peace. One afternoon I stand fingering the small wooden scrolls on the front of the piano while she plays, haltingly, 'The March of the Men of Harlech'. I look at the music, then at her hands, and I see that when the little black dots on the page move up the lines her fingers play nearer the end of the piano.

While she dishes up kumara and home-grown corn in the kitchen I sit on the high piano stool. 'The Men of Harlech' sounds funny with one finger and no flats. My father who sits nearby lowers his newspaper:

'Where there are circles instead of dots, you play the notes longer.'

I look up to see that my mother stands in the doorway with a pot in one hand and a wooden spoon in the other. Her dimples show as she smiles across at me. My joy that day, at learning about music, is not as great as my pleasure at gaining her approval.

I often watch my mother's solitary figure in the garden. She kneels, leaning forward with her feet tucked under. Sometimes I sit in a rectangle of sun on the verandah and stare at her through the white slats. We have a huge garden with our rented house set in the middle. She's cultivated beds of massed petunias, gerberas and zinnias and many other annuals. There are spreading trees in front. Custard apple and mangoes grow down the side too. But I ask her one day why she never plants any of her own. I know she loves magnolias. She says annuals are the best because they're yours for their lifetime. If you plant your favourite trees then you have to leave them behind. But we've lived here forever, so I don't understand.

When she's inside reading, she puts her finger on a word when you speak and you know she'd rather be back in the story. Outside though, she answers in cheerful bursts as she tugs at weeds and flings them behind her for the cats to pounce on. Sometimes in the garden we talk about ghosts and telepathy, and one day I learn that she hears my voice call her name when she's quite alone, just as I have heard hers from somewhere close-by but far away. I told her once, when I was five, that talking to her made me think of a little cobbled path between two cottages – our voices were the path and our heads the little houses. She sat back on her heels that day and hugged me hard. When she does that she caresses my sensibilities and I realise how much more I need to love her than she seems to want or allow.

Most people admire my mother and some are very fond of her. But many only see her cynicism and her eccentricity and regard her with some suspicion. She despises weakness and sentimentality but she shows her own softness in many small ways. On Christmas Day, the cats in a row each have their own treat of anchovy paste which they lick with rasping tongues, moving the tiny tins across the floor as they strive to finish every morsel. On the rare cool nights in Brisbane when fruit bats hang upside down in the Moreton Bay fig trees, she strips our beds and makes little cocoons from the old baby blankets and we curl up in our prickly warm nests while she reads us *Struwelpeter* and poems from the *Child's Garden of Verses.*

We get regular savage beatings with the copper-stick, sometimes for reasons we don't understand or because she's discovered that we've taken sixpence from her purse to buy sweets. She doesn't bear grudges and her tempers, though devastating, are over quickly. But my sister and I can never forget our hurt. It's one of the things that binds us so closely in our childhood relationship of favour, power and fear.

My mother's rules and restrictions seem different from those of the neighbours whose houses we visit after school. Everything's strange there. At their places, shades are drawn against the Brisbane heat. Bottle-green verandah awnings, strapped down, strain and flap in the wind. Inside the darkened rooms, the sense of the neighbours' otherness is exciting yet makes me yearn somehow for home. The smell of old Sunday roast lingers in white net curtains and long brown holland blinds. In these houses the children help themselves to bottled fizzy drinks and biscuits from tins and packets. Bedrooms with huge double-sized beds for two people and white damask spreads, smell of powder and mothballs. Silver-backed hairbrushes rest, bristle sides down, on an angle, on glass topped dressing tables. Instead of sending us quickly out to play as my mother would, we are invited to sit down. We talk together in the dark kitchen with its wooden sink and shelves lined with shiny checked oilcloth. What I notice most of all is that they share their emotions. My mother shows her laughter, her anger or her affection. But somehow it's hers alone.

The gap between my mother and us is greater than in other families. Sometimes the children are allowed to offer advice to the adults and it seems that at those times they're all people. Not children on one side and adults far away on the other. The jokes around other people's tables are not obscure and you don't have to be so careful in what you say.

But my mother lets us do things that others would think scandalous – even helps us at times. Like gathering rotten mangoes to throw at the Sunday school children. We are allowed to walk naked too in our house and garden. If we want to we can go shopping with her, she tells us, minus our clothes. But we never do. On hot days she lets us put thick newspapers under both of the bathroom doors and then fill the bath to overflowing. We call them 'flood baths'. We rub soap all round the wide rim of the old bath then, shining in our nakedness, we sit on the edge and push each other round screaming as we skid and fly. Soap and cold water spray all over the windows and floor and once my little brother breaks his arm. But the latitude she gives us is commensurate with her mood of the moment.

She doesn't talk much about her own mother. But sometimes, on wet afternoons, we sit together on the sofa. She tells us that her maternal grandmother was widowed while very young and devoted herself to the three grandchildren as they arrived. She describes how her granny made buttered eggs and Scotch Broth and often kept her little black-haired granddaughter overnight. They'd eat breakfast together in bed on high embroidered pillows that smelled of lavender. They'd look at Daguerreotypes and make Cats' Cradles from wool. My mother's granny even had a phonograph and cylinders and an old harpsichord. And a picture my mother never forgot, in a golden frame, showing high pink cliffs and down below, watercolour sheep grazing in a pale green landscape and beyond that, a grey sea.

I have recurring nightmares. In them my mother is a determined dark figure riding a cumbersome black motorbike. In the dreams she rides very fast through our house and I run screaming in front of her out of the back door and down the long flight of stairs to the gravel below. When I look back, the motorbike is jolting down each step very efficiently with my mother still seated and inscrutable. I rush to the coal shed and slam the door behind me. After a moment I notice a black crescent appearing under it. The motorbike and its rider have become flat as a page in a book and slowly, as I watch, the front wheel, followed by the rest of the bike, slides further inside. At that point, paradoxically, I wake from my nightmare, screaming for my mother who comes in, thick-voiced with sleep, to comfort me. I know I will never escape her power.

Sometimes I think of the time when I was born, a premature three pounds. I imagine my mother bending over to cradle me in her arms because I was so fragile and not expected to live. She tells me that she said to my father that day:

'I just *can't* lose another – somehow I have the greatest faith that this little one will survive!'

Her shadow falls across me as she sits in her hospital bed – but sometimes I wonder if I'll always live in its darkness.

My older brother is angel-faced and enigmatic. My parents chose him from a Shelter for Fallen Women when he was one year old. After they were married my mother had a baby boy, Roger, who lived for three days and then a year later a little stillborn daughter. The doctors told her she would be unlikely to have any child that would survive. My sister was born two years after she brought my adopted brother home to live. At ten he still wets his pants occasionally and can't learn to play the violin that my mother chose as his hobby. She makes us stand watching the music as he struggles to understand it. She brings our blue mother-of-pearl hairbrushes and instructs us to hit him when he plays a wrong note. We're too frightened to disobey. We stand frozen and anguished in silent never-expressed outrage. Our compassion for him and our alienation from our mother have never been stronger. She doesn't seem to know that he'd play better if she didn't watch. Our mother feels he's slow to read the books she provides and he develops a cowering demeanour that seems to heighten her disapproval and anger toward him. She sends him off periodically to a boys' 'boarding school' in Indooroopilly.

On winter Sundays, while mothball-hail topples off the verandah roof into the flowerbeds below, we look through the huge black embossed photo album that she takes from the top of her wardrobe. Our mother dries rosemary from her back garden between the blank pages at the back. We always like to look first at the green spiky fronds as they lie in such pretty contrast to the dark thick pages. Our mother lets us prise up the miniature branches so we can breathe their bouquet. You can feel with your fingertips the little indents where the sprigs were pressed on the surface of the paper. It's a ritual which holds my sister and me in thrall. It means that we'll soon see the photos. It's strange how you smell things and they remind you. We love to see the pictures of our brother before we knew him. But we're never allowed to turn straight to the pictures of him. The first few pages show the wistful pale-eyed heroes of the Great War. They wear their plumed slouch hats and the photographer has faded out the backgrounds so that they have a sort of misty halo behind their heads.

We attempt to turn the pages impatiently, restlessly kicking our heels on the sofa as our mother lingers over the memories of her girlhood. There are pictures of Burma where she spent several of her later teenage years. There's my grandfather's brother, great uncle Walter. He sits on a verandah wearing plus-fours and dundreary whiskers. Behind him in the shade a butterfly net hangs, teardrop-shaped, on the wall. My sister and I thought, years ago, that it was a bomb descending on him because the photo was taken during the Great War. Steep mountains rise up behind his house and a youth in a loincloth stands to the left holding a basin of water. We fidget and squirm on the sofa beside our mother.

Finally she turns the last page of her young adulthood. At one year old our brother is pink-cheeked and amiable. Pale curls tumble round his chubby neck and shoulders. He wears, then, pintucked handmade suits with frills on the collar and at the wrists. His legs, braceleted with fat, lie on the broderie anglaise coverlet of his pram. Our mother tells us that strangers would stop her at the shops to peer in and to praise his robust beauty. We turn the page to see my father's blurred arms holding him high in mid-toss. And another where they lie face-to-face on a checked rug, foreheads pressed together. My mother stands in the background wearing a felt helmet and a dress almost to the ankles with a swathed bodice and a belt around her hips. A series of deckle-edged pictures show him as a tiny schoolboy in a photographic studio. My sister aged about two and a half sits with her head on his shoulder. Once I touch the sharp, ripply border of one of the photos:

'He looks sad there. Didn't the man give him a boiled sweet like he did for our photo?'

My mother smooths the curling edge which has escaped from its triangular corner:

'Oh, it's a long time ago – I can't remember – I expect he didn't like the bright lights and strange surroundings.'

We watch with sorrow each morning as our brother takes his sheets under the house to the wash-trough. His back trembles with the tears he sheds as he struggles with his heavy burden. His bedroom is a section of latticed verandah with tarpaulins covering it in winter. Here he makes beautiful elaborate Meccano cities. He lets us sit on his camp stretcher to see the dexterity with which he screws the slotted rods together to construct his cranes and skyscrapers. My sister and I watch his face with love for his sweetness of nature and the kindness he shows us. When he goes to stay at the 'boarding school', my mother allows him to take his building set and soft worn toys he still likes to hold in bed.

Usually my father takes him by tram to the bus stop for Indooroopilly. But one day we go too. Standing there in the large warm raindrops that have started to fall, we make our ritualistic promises to marry him when we've all grown up and he smiles at last. Treetops and shop verandahs are reflected on the bus windows as we mime our pledges and goodbyes. We can just discern the pale anxious triangle of his face inside. He sits up at the front near the driver, where they talk of transmissions and the intricacies of internal combustion. The bus leaves in a cloud of black diesel. We know no God at our place but we pray that this time he'll come back continent. My sister uses every penny of her pocket money on sweets for him and the bus fares to visit him whenever she can.

I think my sister's anguish at the hand of my mother turned early from fear to terrrible fury. Through the prism of her rage she watches the world go by with angry eyes. She screams, bites and scratches and lies kicking on the ground over minor issues. She perceives monstrous injustices toward her in the way our mother treats us all. She scrutinises the amount of food that is given to us at meal times to make sure that no one gets one pea more than she does. Her blue eyes are like precision instruments. On Christmas Day of 1940 we receive identical dolls. But my mother hasn't been sufficiently scrupulous in her observation of their tiny voile dresses. Mine has pink, blue and green smocking and my sister's, only pink and blue. She is distraught and hysterical at this seeming favouritism.

Her sensitivity extends into every area of her life, and before she's even started school she has become her own tyrant. She learns to read at three and straddles my father's sawing horse in the sun with a pile of children's books from the library. She is able to hold sophisticated conversations with our parents at an early age, especially with our father. They sit together, blue-eyed and fair-haired and share secrets in words I'll never understand.

At eight she parades her many talents with panache. She climbs the tallest trees. Reads the longest books. And uses the most complicated words with unfailing accuracy. Her vocabulary is both her stock-in-trade and often her undoing. The local children taunt her. They call over our front fence as they pass by:

'You think you're the Queen of Auchenflower.'

My sister looks up from her game of fiddlesticks on the verandah. Her reply is both simple and alienating:

'I don't merely think – I *know*.'

One Sunday evening while we wait for dinner, my sister and I discuss who we'll marry when we're grown up – or rather, our options in case our big brother can't wait for us:

'Well, I'm going to marry the Government.'

I hope to impress my sister with my grasp of current events. My father reads the paper to my mother sometimes while she stirs the groats for breakfast and the Government is frequently mentioned. My sister aged eight replies:

'That's stupid – you can only marry someone *in* the Government.'

And adds unhesitatingly:

'I shall marry the reigning King – that is – if he's suitable.'

Our games with the children in the street are often about the war. Our little brother, aged three, staggers about with a homemade wooden rifle over his shoulder. My sister listens to 'First Light Fraser, a Drama of War-torn Europe', on the radio at five o'clock. It's the story of a spy who is forever being captured by the Nazis and escaping. When neighbouring children come to play she and her friend Rilla Reid organise us into Germans and prisoners. As internees we are lined up with our backs against the custard apple trees. Blindfolds made from tea-towels prevent us from seeing our captors, but we can hear with almost real terror their guttural tones:

'Ze next to die are Fraulein Reid, Fraulein Clark and Herr Richmond.'

A report from our big brother's Daisy air-rifle gives the signal that the firing squad has done its duty and we slump to the ground. An executioner rushes over in her pinafore to push our bewildered little brother so that he too lies groaning and writhing and is finally still. One of the girls pulls a photo of her family from her pocket as she falls and it flutters to the ground beside her. Then it's our turn to be the SS. We decide among ourselves that it's an opportune time for my sister to be sent on a spying mission. She is briefed accordingly and warned that she may be captured by the other side and tortured. The words she utters in spontaneous response make her the heroine of the hour:

'Ze torture, it may be unendurable but it is *nozzing* compared with death.'

My little brother was born three years ago. I can still remember Nurse Collins moving into our house until my mother brought him home. My father seemed to live in his study during that time, only coming out to eat the strange new foods that appeared on our dinner table. While she cooked she sang songs about people being in love. She would let us undo her pageboy hair from its net while she sat in our sitting room, filing her nails and humming her love songs. We would stand behind her to brush and comb the long red tresses. One day we got strips of calico and made Nurse Collins ringlets and a fringe of undulating waves across her forehead. We held up the mirror and she giggled and laughed until her face was wet with tears.

Our big brother would stand close to her after school, talking and helping her make the pudding. He would do anything she asked. He even made his bed without being told. In her room he smoothed the blankets each morning and moved the bed out to tuck in the wall-side sheets. Then he would arrange her pink satin slippers perfectly parallel and fold her nightie under her pillow as he'd watched our mother do. My father asked Nurse Collins politely one night after dinner if she'd had enough to eat and she touched her white throat and laughed:

'Oh yes thank you sir – up to pussy's bow.'

When Nurse Collins was shopping my sister and I would go

into our mother's room to look at the baby's things. In her drawer we saw tiny folded jumpers, not much bigger than dolls' clothes. And pairs of white bootees with ribbon threaded through the ankles and little tight pink rosebuds on the instep part. The ribbons weren't shiny and flat like new ones. My sister told me that my feet would have been the last to be in the bootees. I looked down at my red shoes and couldn't believe her. I smelled the inside of the bootees to see if their scent would remind me of being so tiny. But it didn't. Once we looked in my mother's dressing-table drawer. We found a dark tan rubber ball with a little hose attached. Other complicated tubes lay alongside. And some ointment with the bottom flattened and creased from being used. But our father came in then and when he saw what we were doing, his face was suddenly serious. He pulled our hands away from the interesting box and shut the drawer firmly:

'Those are mummy's *private* things – off you go now!'

My father brought the pram out from under the house and hosed it. Then he rubbed Velvet soap on a brush and scrubbed it. All over the inside and outside of the cream-painted cane. He gave us old rags and we helped to dry it before wheeling it up onto the verandah. He told us that, because the new baby was premature, it would be as tiny as my doll, Katriona. He spread one hand and hollowed it a little to show us how he could hold our new brother in his palm quite comfortably.

Then at last my mother came home with the baby. At first its screaming in the middle of the night worried and woke me. I helped to bath him. I prodded tentatively at the tiny bobbing tip that floated on the water between his legs. It was so tender and sweet I drew back surprised:

'It's so soft – what is it?'

I knew. But I wanted her to say. She didn't look at me:

'It's his tail of course.'

His tail! So that's what they were called. But why not at the back like other tails? At last I had a doll that moved and felt warm. I was allowed to hold him and sometimes when I fed him, my lap would suddenly be hot and wet.

My mother let him lie in his big pram in the shade of the mango tree on warm days. I remember once, when I was in the garden and the sky was blue as my mother's delphiniums, the bottoms of the kitchen curtains licked in and out in the wind like someone signalling. I approached the pram. It was jiggling a little on its leather straps so I knew my baby brother had woken from his sleep. I lifted the fine green net which bunched to nothing in my hand. At three months old, he had the navy-blue eyes of the very young infant. His long eyelashes had their cup-shaped shadow where the inner corner of his eye met the curve of his nose. He looked beyond my face at something, blinking and smiling as he stared upward. I followed his gaze to see the reflections of the mango leaves dancing on the net above him. With my head in the pram, so close to my baby brother – and the green material around my shoulders, I sniffed the sweetness of his milky cheek. I remember the wind changed that day and the sun went in with all the capriciousness of a summer's day. And my baby brother cried with disappointment that his magic lantern had disappeared forever.

When he was ten months and crawling we used to have races up and down the verandah on our hands and knees. We would laugh so much, one day he was sick in a little milky patch of curds and whey. I would haul him onto my lap and kiss his sweet-smelling cheek. Once I bit it. Quite hard. And that was interesting because I found I could make him cry. But I was always sorry. I could make him sleep too by jogging his pram. I would dress him in my big sleeping-doll's knitted dresses and bootees and bonnets. My mother was angry once because all you could see was his round surprised face, red and beaded all over with a spray of perspiration.

Later, when he walked, I'd take his small fat star-shaped hand. He'd stumble along beside me, falling down every few minutes. Once he ate a geranium and his face clenched and shuddered at the taste. We shared the nursery and I'd wake him early to have his gentle company before I was allowed to get up. He'd suck on last night's bottle and then give me a turn. I'd hug him so hard that he'd look frightened for a moment. I wished that he would never grow up.

Now he's older I like it when we play war together. We crouch with our wooden guns behind the ringed and knotted trunks of the camphor laurels, in our matching checked overalls. He comes with me to the infant school and we have to stop calling him 'Taffy' and use his real name. At home I set out the rows of glossy shells that will help him learn to count in the coming months. He puts his name in mirror writing on his many drawings. At school they tie his left hand to the desk so he'll learn to write with the other one. But his left is his drawing hand at home and after a few months the teachers give up.

My younger brother is my dearest friend. I admire my sister and feel a very strong bond – almost as if she's another aspect of myself – but I can't predict her moods so I can't trust her.

For my older brother I feel love and great compassion.

My mother is frightening, unfathomable darkness. I yearn to get close to the tenderness I know is there.

And my father? Like an astronomer adjusting the telescope's focus, then peering at some distant moon, I catch sometimes a glimpse of his bright outline, but usually he's blurred and remote.

4
FRIENDS AND NEIGHBOURS

A stroll across the garden, past the air-raid shelter and through our mother's legendary vegetable garden takes us to the Misses Mills. They're our neighbours and they live with their father, a clergyman, and their old cream labrador who has eyes like holes burned in blankets. The Misses Mills both wear glasses and my mother says she never knows them apart. But then, she hasn't sat for hours over afternoon tea with them while the clocks tick at different paces, the dog snuffles as close as he dares to the cream-puffs, and the Reverend Mills clickety clacks his sermon in the parlour down the hall.

At the Misses Mills we sip from unaccustomed cups – and you couldn't put a pin between the roses on them. The sugar in the crystal bowl is white. Not the brown sort our mother uses – which moves almost imperceptibly long after you've dipped your spoon in it. Both the sugar bowl and the pale green plaster vase of flowers sit on crocheted doilies, the colour of sunburned knees. Sometimes I stare at the mauve and magenta blooms so carefully arranged by one of the Misses Mills and I try hard to hate the colours, when really they're the most beautiful I've ever seen. My mother says that any colour belonging to the purple family is vulgar. The biscuits we eat at the Misses Mills come from a tin with a parrot on the front. When you open the hinged lid you can smell metal and see your smudged reflection.

One afternoon, the Reverend Mills, having finished his sermon early, comes in to share our bread and butter and to tap his barometer. With a benevolent smile at my sister, he asks her if she'd like to see how a typewriter works. My sister, with a glance at me which gives me gooseflesh, disappears into the gloomy recesses of the passage. Five minutes later she returns minus the

Reverend Mills and her face reveals nothing except a faint smile. It's only when we're home, having clambered through the macrocarpa hedge (to boast that our feet didn't touch the ground from the Misses Mills to home) that I ask her if she was allowed to type anything herself. She takes a piece of ice-blue, religious-looking paper from her pocket and I read:

> *Roses are red, violets are blue*
> *If my bum's pink then yours is too.*

Our mother sits with her glass of sherry in one hand and her *New Yorker* open on her knees as the radio plays the Wilfred Thomas theme. I can hear my father working across the hall in his study. The smell of his pipe hangs in the air. Each time my mother uncrosses her legs or turns a page, the cats' eyes open suddenly wide. They lie sleeping temporarily at this time of day, or pretending to rest to conceal their anxiety. When she moves to put her glass down and to smooth open the silky new pages of her magazine, the cats give a token stretch and are at the door with moist meows. We sit waiting for the right moment and when our mother looks up to ask about our tea party next door, we show her the poem, now sticky with macrocarpa juice. She laughs very loudly and throws back her shiny, black hair. Then, to the cats' delight she jumps up to show our father in his study.

Her laughter reminds me of another summer evening when I rushed in hot-cheeked with importance from my first Band of Hope class. They were held in the church above the school next door and promised sophistication beyond the dreams of most five year olds. I came home that night with my own personal pledge on stiff parchment that smelled of the church incense. The teacher taught us to read it:

> *I promise, God helping me, to abstain from*
> *all intoxicating liquors, as beverages and to*
> *get others to do the same.*

I'd sat in the hedge to memorise it. My father removed his pipe from the side of his mouth that night to shout with laughter as my mother poured herself a large sherry and drained it, dancing back and forth over the precious parchment until it was sodden and unrecognisable. I joined the laughter but my throat ached with tears.

Sometimes we visit Ethel Quinn who lives in the street at the back of the Misses Mills. Valerie Quinn is one of my sister's school-friends. Our mother tells us that Ethel Quinn's husband, Dave, gets things on the black market, which sounds sinister. But to see him, you'd never guess. He looks just like an ordinary father, with a white shirt and braces and old pinstriped trousers. The police called one day when we were there. They took away some cigarette lighters that Dave Quinn dug up for them from a tin in the backyard while the police stood by and watched. My mother takes a notebook and often writes what Ethel Quinn says, so she can show my father later.

The Quinns live in a small house close to the footpath. There's a tiny garden in front. An arbour of roses curves over the wire gate. The tiles on the verandah have a name – Edwin – set into them in a much darker colour. It could be the name of the man who built the house. Or perhaps the father of a little girl who lived there long ago. The tin roofed verandah runs the width of the house to shade the windows of the two front bedrooms and the front door. At right-angles to it are brown wooden arches of differing sizes.

Sometimes, before I cross the road with my mother and sister, to Ethel Quinn's, I like to stand and look at her picture-book cottage. I always start from the right hand archway over the bedroom window. Little arch . . . wide arch . . . little arch. Then a medium one over the front door. The small ones are half the size of the widest and the one medium curve is somewhere in between . . . so two baby ones equal one big and the medium equals . . .

'Come on! What on earth are you *doing* over there – no, look *both* ways, you foolish child!'

My mother stands just inside Ethel Quinn's front entrance. Her face is shaded and her arm which holds back the wire door, is striped with the sun that shines through the wooden toast racks above the arches. I walk through the arbour and down the tiny cement path with its border of upright terracotta tiles and stiff zinnias beyond. Then up a small flight of steps. The exercise book she keeps for Ethel Quinn's sayings, peeps from her old leather bag. She puts her hand out, rough and prickly from gardening, to draw me inside with a half-caress to the back of my neck:

'You spend your life in another world – one day I'll wake and find that you've flown away there in the night.'

The front door of the Quinns' is usually propped open by a chipped plaster spaniel of life size – one eye closed in a wink. On either side of the narrow front hall are bedrooms with the blinds drawn. The rooms have painted wooden ceilings and small ornate metal fireplaces with grates that are never used. In one, iceland poppies glow, made by Ethel Quinn from crepe paper. Then the passage ends in an archway which is flanked by two narrow dark green velvet curtains. You push through these and find yourself in the dining room which the Quinns seem to live in. A round table is covered with a lace cloth the colour of wheatmeal biscuits. A bay window on the left curves out into the side garden. Its sills, when you look behind the lace curtain, are littered with the dried bodies of long-dead flies. The furniture in here is huge and dark and the sideboard has a Toby jug and some dusty cups and saucers that are too good to use. A china cabinet with glass doors, houses slim-stemmed crystal goblets – amethyst, with etched designs. They too, are never brought out – instead, Ethel Quinn's friends drink from plain glasses that once held Vegemite or mayonnaise.

The kitchen next to this room, is all pale green and cream with a louvred window that looks onto the back garden. When you stand on tip toe to peep out, you see through the dusty glass slats some grass, a swing and an old kennel. Up at the back near the neighbour's fence, grow rows of blue cabbages that look from here like a rectangle of back-to-front knitting.

Ethel Quinn is everybody's picture of a closet alcoholic. In the dining room, she pours from a teapot full of gin. Her cup on an angle, she keeps the spout well hidden from our view. My mother likes coffee so a bottle of Turban Essence is set before her with a cut-glass jug of milk. We eat the sardine sandwiches that Ethel Quinn's made for morning tea and drink our powdered milk cocoa, while we listen at her table. Her staring, blue eyes rheumy with their constant trickle of sorrow, she tells us a confusion of anecdotes about her cat, Lady, that died from a bait and her eldest daughter, Violet, who fell pregnant by a soldier and went to live in the West. She sips from her cup then puts it down with both hands to steady it:

'Dave doesn't love me anymore – he's as good as told me – he treats me like I was a dog.'

She hesitates and looks our way, then back to our mother. Fingers fanned beside her mouth in unsuccessful secrecy, she leans toward our mother and says in her hoarse voice:

'Last winter he moved into Violet's old bedroom,' and takes up her cup again to sip away her sadness and to continue:

'It's hard to look in the mirror when you know no one loves you – even your own kids treat you like dirt – and your neck's starting to go too.'

I look across at her with some alarm. But Ethel Quinn's neck is still there alright. My mother jots surreptitiously in her exercise book.

As the gin soothes her grief, she forgets about concealing the spout of the teapot and we watch the liquid pour as clear as her teardrops. She tells us our hair will sap our strength and stunt our growth if it's not kept cut above the ear lobes; that you treat carbuncles by drawing them first with a sock filled with hot sand, then attacking them with a scrubbing brush; how her friend Nesta Trimm had watched her own children drown when their canoe overturned in the Brisbane River, and just one year later had choked to death on a caramel while crossing the Story

Bridge; and how her cousin's best friend was stabbed in the stomach by an Aborigine. She chronicles the mishaps in her family, tracing their tragedies back to 1854. Then, flushed and almost incoherent, she sings the chorus from 'The Bonnie Banks of Loch Lomond'. She lifts a crossed pair of swords from the wall and dances an unsteady hornpipe. Wiping the moist moustache on her upper lip with the back of her hand, she sits to pant and to dry her face on the corner of the lace cloth. My sister and I can't take our eyes off her hair with its nits that traverse the greying curls. Poor Ethel Quinn hiccups enormously – the sort my little brother gives after he's had a tantrum. She weaves her way through to the kitchen and across to the louvred window. It opens with a sharp click and she calls out placatingly:

'Did you want your tea now, love? It's made.'

Dave Quinn must have answered or gestured his reply because she shuts the slats with a rasping noise and returns to the dining room:

'Suit y'self, you stupid lookin' arrangement – you can stay out there all day and night for all I care,' and turns directly to my mother: 'You'd think I'd offered him arsenic – he's that rude to me. 'Course sometimes he'll bring home a paira silk stockings he's picked up at the pub.'

She glances at us, then back to my mother: 'But I know it's because he wants his bitta liberty with me that night.'

She pours again from the teapot and raises her cup before drinking:

'Victory – and our lads' safe return!'

With this justification, she drains the cup.

We leave with Ethel Quinn through the back door. Dave Quinn looks up weasel-like then back to his digging. She wants to show us her sweet peas. They weave through the white trellis in pastel abundance and tiny green tendrils the shape of possums' tails brush the earth below. She stops to stroke the flared transparency of a bloom recently opened then steps round the corner ahead of us to walk down the side of the house. Beneath the bay window of the dining room there's a wide spread of pink and white jasmine. Like a valance. It grows to sill height then each laden branch curves downward again. The air along here is permeated with its sweet smell. If you blur your eyes, it's like a beautiful ballerina's skirt with the ends trailing gracefully in a fan shape through the nasturtiums in the garden bed underneath. My mother comments and stops to stare. Ethel Quinn, who's ahead, looks over her shoulder then walks unsteadily back:

'Would you like a slip or two of me little darlin's? Not that there's much these days.'

She goes looking for the secateurs.

'Whew! You could ignite her breath with one of Dave's cigarette lighters,' laughs my mother, her eyes still on the fall of jasmine. Ethel Quinn returns:

'There you are, love, you take what you want – put them in a sunny spot. Every time you look at them you can remember Ethel.'

We pass purple bougainvillea on our left, that towers taller than my mother. Some bushes of lantana brush our bare legs. You can smell aniseed from the pelargoniums that dip through the lattice between the stilts of the house. My mother bends slightly as she passes through the rose arbour. My sister is close beside her. I follow behind. Now on the cracked asphalt footpath, I look back. I notice in the right hand side of the tiny front garden something I didn't see on my way in. A cement bird-bath – moss-covered and almost hidden by long grasses. And at its base, a circlet of lobelias in their stained-glass hues. Testimony to the poetry once present in Ethel Quinn before the gin and tears and the lost illusions.

5
BOGGABILLA

In 1942 our parents tell us that Japanese soldiers have bombed Darwin. They decide that my sister and I should be evacuated to the country in the south for a few months until the danger to Brisbane passes. No one under six is allowed to go so our little brother, aged four, will stay home. Our older brother can't come with us either. He's in the 'boarding school' again. We beg unsuccessfully for him to return and to be evacuated with us but our mother says he'll be sent with the school elsewhere.

Several weeks later my sister and I leave for Boggabilla – a country toy-town set flat on ochre plains in New South Wales; one narrow bitumen road snakes through, past hotel, general store and a peeling timber chapel. A dog urinates against the door of the scout hall then hurtles off alarmed when our bus approaches across a paddock in a cumulus of yellow dust. Inside, the hall is dark and the wooden floors echo to the pigeon-feathered rafters with our voices and the turmoil of cases and bags dumped by the driver. The double timber doors sway and creak in the cool New South Wales wind.

The women who will care for us for three months drag kitchen equipment and cases of food up the steps onto the stage. Here, a row of rusty primus cookers provides a makeshift kitchen. There are meat safes that squeak and swing in the shade outside on the long timbered southern wall, and sentinel coolgardies for the milk and butter. My sister and I clutch our dolls and books and stay close together. At seven, I'm one of the youngest evacuees. Hessian hangs gigantically from beams to separate boys' and girls' sleeping quarters. Our beds are rows of camp stretchers. In the months that follow, some will tilt and teeter in the winter morning winds outside where they're placed to be hosed and to lean and dry. Even the older children, separated for so long from their families, have accidents at night.

The porridge we eat each day is made from maize boiled with powdered milk. It has suds on the top. We eat from tin bowls that clatter as loud as the corrugated sheets on the roof in the windy evenings. The bread that's cut in hurried wedges by our caregivers each meal time, comes from a tiny bakery a mile away. The children, in twos, take it in turns to run each morning up the slippery, winter road to fetch it. Coming home, we hug the hot loaves and sniff their acrid black crusts. The bravest dig out the moist, yeasty centre, their breath misting back behind them as they run. Once, when it's my turn to go, there's a cold wind which makes my ears ache like a drill in the centre of my head. Weeping with the pain on my way home, I press warm pellets of the fresh dough as far as I can inside my ears.

Grey laundry troughs stand in one section of the scout hall's yellow paddock. Once a week they're filled with warm water brought by the lumbering, staggering women and some of the older boys. Partitions from the nearby church stand on the stubbly grass around each trough and the smaller children are bathed first. We run screaming, naked and pink, back to our clothes inside.

The day the post is due to arrive we wake early. Our mother has sent a parcel for each of us. My sister has two books – *What Katy Did Next* and *The Good Master*. I find in mine, drawing paper and a skein of pink and silvery-grey flecked wool. I wrote to our mother three weeks ago to tell her that I'd learned to knit and needed wool for my doll's jumper. I miss her suddenly, as I open my package and cry when I think of her choosing such a beautiful colour.

In July we hire a bus and picnic in a faraway pine forest. In contrast to the bright day, it's dark and the reflections of our voices are suddenly dulled as we enter. Inside it smells of fresh sap and the fragrance of the prickly branches that tear at our hair as we run. We have three-legged competitions, sack jumping and relay races. I'm disconcerted when someone urgently hands me a short, cylindrical stick. I look at it and people around me are leaping up and down and screaming:

'Run *back* – go on, stupid, run *back*!'

The women hang apples from the high branches and we have to try to be first to eat them, with our hands tied behind our backs. The bus driver brings the rubbish tin from the boot and we gather our crusts and apple cores till it's full. We stand the bin on the slippery tan pine needles that coat the forest floor and take it in turns to jump over. Terry Hamilton is eight and we know he's delicate because the women take special care with him, but he wants to jump too. He almost clears the rubbish tin but his inside thigh catches on the handle and blood spurts and throbs down his leg and into his sandshoe. The women lie him down and quickly put their hankies and scarves against his wound. We crowd round him looking first at his white face then back to the anxious pallor of the women. The scarves and hankies colour deep red and even the ground he lies on as he grows paler is scarlet too. We pack up and leave the pine forest quickly. The women group up the front with the driver and talk with soft urgency as he drives, while we sit subdued and wondering in the hush of the bus. We stop at the Bush Hospital ten miles before Boggabilla and Terry Hamilton is carried inside for transfusions. Back at the scout hall, Mrs Englart takes the stage that night and we learn about haemophilia.

On a warm, late-winter's day, we take a bus to the dry Dumaresq river bed, miles from Boggabilla. We pass miniature townships. The inhabitants wave to us from their windows and the post and rail fences they lean on. The sky above them is mottled with clouds. Outside a wooden pub an old man with a greasy felt hat and trousers tied at the knee with string, looks up slowly. He raises his pot of beer in salute. Nearby is a small dog. His whole body jolts forward rhythmically and his mouth opens and shuts. Because our windows are shut and the bus is noisy, we can't hear his bark. A line of wind-break pines on a hill tapers to the crest then vanishes down the other side. We arrive at the riverbank and the boys slide down the slopes on the seats of their serge pants. Small stones scatter and fly as they descend. We find that we can draw faces with pieces of chalky rock, on the hard, pink banks that rise up ten and twelve feet around us. When I look up from my drawing, I see a multitude of pastel colours – a china blue sky, the old-rose of the streaky walls nearby and olive greens of ghost gums tossing far above. Even a neat flock of pink and grey parakeets leaves one tree in a soft spray, to settle in another. The women have brought tomato sandwiches and cold potatoes from last night's fire. We finish our meal with watermelon that I bring up later through the bus window on the way home.

On cold evenings the older children light camp fires in the stubbly field near the scout hall and we sit round singing songs of soldiers returning from the war, while our shins scorch in the heat and our calves stay cool. Imelda Englart throws sweet potatoes into the embers and an hour later we nibble at the hot, mealy outsides then crunch the uncooked centres. The teenage children sing 'Izzy an' Ozzie, izzy Lizzy' and 'Lily of Laguna'. One fuzzy-chinned youth, given courage by the relative darkness, acts out the words as he sings:

> *'Don't tear my heart, like it was paper,*
> *Don't say sweet things when they're not true.'*

On Sunday mornings the women wash our hair if the day is sunny, then dab our scalps with kerosene. They then proceed to pull out lice and eggs. Relentless, fine-toothed combs rake our heads as we crouch over enamel basins. With stinging scalps and faces streaked with tears we sit one by one in a row against the splintery timber walls of the hall. At least the itching will stop till the next infestation.

Pocket money sent to the women by our parents, is doled out each Saturday. There is never any debate about how it will be spent. We make straight for the General Store whose range of lollies is almost as limited as the amount we are all given to spend. At home our mother kept the occasional sweet for rewards if we hadn't bitten our nails that week or for when we fell over and skinned a knee. But here there are chocolate Buddies by Sweetacres (ten for a penny), sherbet in a small waxed bag with a narrow licorice straw and more. By the time the youngest of us arrive, the pickings are slim. I buy four rejected ginger hearts that never taste of ginger and a lock-jaw toffee bar called a Kurl.

Some of the children flushed with Saturday excitement and the power of the sixpenny pieces that remain as testimony of restraint in the fuzz at the bottom of their pockets, decide to swim in the winter water of the Macintyre River. David and Kevin Ferguson, twins from Eliot's Landing, say they are going to break the ice. I follow them down to the water's edge, devising in my head ways to construct makeshift skates. I arrive breathless but although my eyes flick up and down the river for several minutes, I see no ice. None of the other children seem surprised at this and they follow the twins who are in the water now, shouting with the cold. I walk back home alone and eat the last of my ginger hearts on my bed with someone's dog-eared copy of *Film Fun*.

We go by bus to a village nearby for our schooling. At first, the local children there call us 'reffoes'. They snigger, nudge and spit when we approach them. The school is tin-roofed and stands on stilts. Before the day's lessons, our teacher steps to the front of the class and beats time with her arms while we're instructed to sing:

> *'Good morning to you,*
> *Good morning to you,*
> *Good morning, dear tea-cher,*
> *We're glad to see you.'*

We make rows of pencilled pot-hooks and learn from readers with steel-engraved illustrations. Little Gertrude wears a frilled bonnet and pinny and her behaviour in the stories is exemplary. We read about children who sin and about the retribution they receive. On the wall of the classroom a faded sepia poster depicts a dark-haired man with a shine across his neat, short hair. He has a thin moustache and wears a white coat. From his gleaming lips, a speech bubble bears the legend: 'Nowadays, dentists know the importance of fresh fruit.' I love the word 'nowadays' though I've never seen or heard it before. I have a sense of anachronism about it. I think I know what it would mean. My composition begins:

'Nowadays, I don't live with my mother and father . . .'

Sometimes I think with wonder of our high-stilted house back in shady-treed Munro Street – the quiet symmetry of its return verandah and the cool of its lofty pressed-metal ceilings. Time there seems suspended, like the dragon-flies that hover over Auchenflower's hedges. I remember my mother, dark-haired and long-aproned. She stands at the stove or kneels by her circular flower-bed. Weeds are strewn around her in my memory as she talks to herself under the Brisbane sun. I miss the stories at night on her lap or in bed and I think of the big white bath on lion's legs. But my stomach contracts when I remember her sudden, black rages when she knocks us to the floor for mysterious misdemeanours and the whippings with the copper stick which leave our bottoms and thighs bruised black for weeks. When we read one morning in our letters that she's missing us and will visit Boggabilla with our little brother I feel disquietude at the turmoil of conflict in my head.

It's two and a half months since we've seen our mother. Her precise New Zealand accent strikes us first. When we greet her with stories of our new lives in the country she says:

'Children! Your *voices!* I can't believe it! My angels have turned into little Australians!'

We stay a further three weeks and my mother becomes one of the women who slave over Irish stew up on the stage in the scout hall. In early September we leave Boggabilla's empty paddocks and sparse stands of wattle. My sister and I kiss the stage steps, the unsteady doors of the hall and the old untuned piano that provided so many impromptu concerts. Our breath frosting the bus windows, we wave to the little group of assembled shopkeepers and return the way we came so long ago.

6
TAMBORINE MOUNTAIN

It's the first day of the new year – January the first, 1943. The taxi is due at half past twelve and our father is doing his final check of the windows and doors. He nails pieces of wood where the French doors meet. Our mother stands in a corral of cases, hands on her hips:

'For God's sake Norman, will you stop! We have nothing to pinch and anyway we'll only be gone for a fortnight.'

We sit in a row on the broad flight of wooden steps that spans the space from front path to front verandah. When you look between your knees you can see, through dark lattice, the huge cool space beyond. All the houses in Auchenflower have stilts and lattice. Underneath you find cement wash-troughs and green-flecked coppers for wash days and perhaps a rope clothes line or two. Huge wicker prams and broken bicycles lean against each other, swathed in cobwebs. The farthest fronds of lantana and japonica push through from outside.

My mother, in the sun, is opening a tin of camp pie, her arm jolting up and down like a steam piston. She presses back the ragged lid and with a stick which she washes under the tap, she divides the contents into five and scrapes it onto giant Moreton Bay fig leaves that my father has gathered from the tree near the front gate:

'Now children,' she says, 'you are in a restaurant in Spain, overlooking the sea. The waiter has just served you his special delicacy – devilled ham in vine leaves and he expects you to eat every bit – except the leaves.'

Our father stands in the middle of Munro Street, hands in his tweed trouser pockets and scans the distance for signs of the cab. Our early lunch over, my mother licks her handkerchief and wipes the traces of food from our chins. I sometimes notice other mothers doing the same as they walk their children home from school but in their families, the children, not the mother, lick the hanky. She takes our little brother behind a bush for a minute, as the car draws up and the driver swings the cases on top and secures them with leather straps.

Tamborine Mountain lies five hours away and our taxi drops us in town at the bus terminus. Our father rubs a pound note several times between finger and thumb, to make sure it's not two, and hands it to the driver. Brisbane is hot and dusty in January and the bitumen shimmers and mirages in the distance as we watch through the bus windows and feel the thud of each case as it lands in the boot.

Our father lights his pipe and our little brother, seated on his knee, blows out the proffered match. My sister and I sit together, having promised not to quarrel. She's next to the window but half way we'll swap and I'll have the window seat till Tamborine. The bus lurches forward. Our mother takes out her knitting.

After an hour we travel beside yellow paddocks and I lean back and watch telegraph wire loop and disappear and loop again, the poles flashing past with mesmeric regularity. I look across the aisle at my father. His paper is half on his lap and half on the floor. He sleeps with his head back on bottle green leather and his mouth wide open. My brother slumps against his chest and slumbers too. My mother sits behind us. I can hear her talking intermittently in her resonant voice to someone beside her. Now and then she laughs loudly. There are small gaps in their conversation. Then her companion remarks on a group of sheep with their lambs or a particularly verdant patch of pasture and my mother's knitting needles click endlessly like muted machinery.

At half past three we begin the ascent to the top of Mount Tamborine. The road winds and curves and throws us gently against each other with every hard turn of the steering wheel. Some of the passengers start singing 'Lily of Laguna' and 'Keep the Home Fires Burning'. A man sitting in front of us rustles paper and suddenly thrusts a bag of peppermints over the back of his seat. We suck hard to stop our ears popping. We look out on darkly green foliage close by as the road winds up through stands of towering trees and just as suddenly, emerges to patches of startling daylight. Huge leaves brush and scratch at the windows as the afternoon grows cooler. The gears shudder and swallow and we drop back to a crawling pace on a stretch of steep incline, as silent mountain rain briefly mists the windows and we near the summit.

At the top the evening is clear and all the roads and tracks up here are richly tangerine. I thought the top of the mountain would be a small hump, but there are rutted roads and fenced off houses in paddocks and quite open green countryside. Even the air in the bus now smells of eucalypt and we can see exotic, unfamiliar flowers in the pockets of vegetation by the roadside.

The driver stops near a track that leads off to a weatherboard farmhouse some distance away. This is Callaghan's cottage and it belongs to a friend of our parents. We stand ankle-deep in blue chocolate flowers by the side of the road. The bus rumbles on to its next destination across the mountain top. We can hear a waterfall in the distance and the call of birds we haven't heard before. You have a feeling of height up here because of the strange horizons and the sky seems closer. At home in Auchenflower there's always something in the distance, usually a building, but here, in places there's nothing. Just blue sky that dips down the sides of the mountain.

The cottage is small and my parents have one bedroom while the three of us share another. The kitchen has a fuel stove and a square table with lino tacked on top. A calendar from last year, showing April, hangs behind the door and there's a picture of a soldier in camouflage with a bayonet. He crouches threateningly amid greenery. Underneath, I can just read its caption with some difficulty – 'Jungle fighting's touch'. I puzzle over this, knowing better than to ask my sister who knows everything. Some days later, I put my celluloid doll among an arrangement of leaves in a vase. I write a small notice, saying 'Jungle fighting's touch'. I overhear my mother say to my father:

'Oh, look Norman, "Jungle fighting's tough" – how priceless!'

For me, the mystery is finally solved.

The cottage has a sitting room with a pianola which we are forbidden to play – except when my parents are out on their evening stroll. Once when my mother is picking wildflowers, my father sits and plays 'Tales from the Vienna Woods'. He jumps up, embarrassed, when he sees her returning. The windows in the sitting room look out on long tawny grass that stretches to the forest edge about half a mile away. After dinner, in the no-man's-land between toad-in-the-hole and bed, I sit reading the *Tailor of Gloucester* while my sister pushes our brother on the wooden swing outside. The sprinkle of their voices fuses with the crackle of the seven o'clock news. A little brown bakelite radio that looks like tortoiseshell, sits on the bookshelf next to my father's chair. Dark brown fabric peeps between the slats of the speaker and the dial glows yellow in the half-light. I look up to ask my father what catastrophe means and as I talk, I notice that his eyes match exactly the blue curtains just behind him. The velvet is bleached in the folds which catch the light. I cross the room to finger their incredible softness. I wonder if my mother has ever thought about velvet for our sitting room at home, but when I suggest it, hesitating because of her omniscience, she replies:

'Velvet for curtains is bourgeois.'

I despair of ever equalling her knowledge and I blush as I return to my book.

On a day when you can feel the stillness of Tamborine's morning and magpies call to punctuate absolute silence, I see from bed my father cross the garden with a scythe from the cobwebs in the shed. He is making the grass round the cottage snakeproof. I can catch fragments of sound now from the kitchen as my mother stokes the stove for breakfast. I sit up and watch the rhythmic strokes of my father's labour. Suddenly he stops and shouts, then starts hopping about on one leg. I hear a clatter from the kitchen, and my mother in her apron is running to him. I can just discern through the waist-high grass, my father's arm round her neck as she half carries, half drags him toward the kitchen. I stand out of bed, still at the window and the urine is hot as it pours down my legs and soaks the autumn tones of the carpet. I watch through the hinges in the kitchen door as my mother bathes my father's gashed shin and wraps it in tea-towels. The socks around my ankles grow clammy. Later, I hide the wet pants and socks in bushes far beyond the house. We're told over breakfast that when our father saw the blood, he fainted. He can't even bear the sight of women's hands when they're wearing red nail-polish.

When he's better we make an expedition to a rain forest far from Callaghan's cottage. My mother stays back with my brother whose legs are too short to walk far. Compared with the hot, dry day outside, the forest feels cool and steamy and the tangled vines and leaves, so far above, provide a sort of aviary which shades and dapples. A narrow track, soft with fallen leaves winds for miles. Parrots fly frighteningly low. I can almost feel their wings brush my cheek. The sounds of the forest are contained and echoless. Everything in here is magnified – my father's voice, with its tapering sentences as he strides ahead calling back and the tramp of our feet on damp foliage – even the slow fall of a forest leaf. My father warns us to watch for snakes that may lie curled across the track and, to my relief, he starts loudly singing 'Soup of the Evening, Beautiful Soup' to frighten them. I hope snakes aren't deaf. I hope those little holes they have on their heads are ears. We sit on our jumpers that my father takes from his rucksack and eat my mother's shortbread, while we listen to the still sounds around us. My father folds a shiny leaf then and tries to play 'In Dulci Jubilo' on it, while my sister and I fall about with laughter. I suck the salty butter from the shortbread and wish this day would last forever.

In the mornings, at Callaghan's cottage, we make toast by spearing bread with long-handled forks and expose it to the little open door of the fuel stove. At home, cream is rationed and often unobtainable. Up here we spread our toast with strawberry jam and a thick blanket of yellow cream that my mother doesn't even have to whip. We buy food twice a week from the village an hour and a half away. The road is grooved; and red and dusty, with frequent cowpats. Iridescent flies, that cling to the crusts of the mounds, scatter when we poke the hard ridged exteriors with sticks, to expose the creamy, jungle-green inside. My mother pulls the iron pushcart behind her. A small cemetery signals the last lap of our trek to the shops and after two or three trips we know the names of the dead by heart.

At three o'clock we eat afternoon tea at the Hotel St Bernard which has a beer garden at the back. Our parents buy us marzipan 'potatoes', rolled in cocoa, to eat – while they sip their drinks under striped umbrellas. Released, we run beside clipped hedges – fragrant, yet somehow disturbing, with their privet smell. On the lawn at the front of the Hotel St Bernard is a small red-painted rotunda. Its conical wooden ceiling increases then diminishes the sounds of our voices as we run back and forth inside. My sister stands very still in the centre, looking up. Then exclaims:

'Oh! – it's acoustics!'

I lean on the railing, hot sun on my back and watch her. I think she's imagining how her violin would sound. At home she plays a tune called Rubinstein's 'Melody in F' which my mother hates. She learns to please her teacher by making the music sound poignant and sorrowful. She swoops from one note to the next in a dramatic agony of sentimentality. Sometimes she exaggerates the mood of the pieces so much, that my mother says:

'I dare you to play it just like that for Miss Meadows.'

My sister always wins first prize in the concerts and there are tears in her teacher's eyes. I duck under the railing that smells of hot paint and lie in the dark shade at the base of the rotunda. With springy grass at my back and the faraway sounds as the others play, I lie and watch the teased-out strands of clouds as they hang horizontally above. Some of them remind me of curdled junket where they thin out to nothingness. The voices stop and begin as sounds do when you cover and uncover your ears.

On the way back home, my brother sits in the red pushcart and we take turns to push him the long route home. My father makes incomprehensible jokes and, flushed from his visit to the beer garden, sings songs from the 'St Matthew Passion'. He hugs my mother so hard she says:

'That's enough Norman.'

He teaches us the words from 'The Ash Grove' and we sing while he harmonises with the bass part:

'I'll be the tenor and you girls be the fivers.'

It's the only joke of his I understand, so I laugh too long.

When it's my turn to push the cart, I look at my brother reclining inside. He's big enough, at five, that his elbows stick out and his knees bend up. His sandalled brown feet rest on the dimpled metal foot-rest. I remember, long ago, when I sat there too, watching tree trunks and flowers as they passed me and clouds that followed wherever I went. My mother and father stop for a rest and my sister and I draw with long sticks in the red dust. Our battlement castles and whiskered cats, together with our names, fan away in the next wind. A wild mountain pig with tapering hindquarters scuttles across the track and sends us screaming to the protective folds of our mother's skirt.

My sister made a chart yesterday, which she pinned to the fly-spotted wall next to our beds at Callaghan's cottage. It reads:

> *Days left – two*
> *Number of hours – 48 including bus trip home*
> *Number of minutes – 2,880*
> *Number of seconds – 172,800.*

Meticulously, she crosses off the hours as they pass and after each cross she draws a tiny, sad face with a tear on its cheek. On the second last night in bed, we tell each other stories with plots drawn heavily from the *Green Fairy Book*. We challenge each other to study the chart and when our melancholy becomes unbearable, we defocus our eyes till its numbers and crying faces become a blur. On the day before we're due to leave, we take a picnic by bus to Curtis Falls.

We hear the boom of the water from far away and when we arrive we have to cover our ears until the shock of its thunder becomes part of the day. A small path through moist-leaved undergrowth leads us closer and suddenly we're in a clearing. The falls are only twenty feet away on the other side. They drop sheerly out of a sky that's almost turquoise in contrast. The scene that confronts us is overwhelming and the three of us hang behind. Our parents move forward to find a place to sit and spread the rug, out of range of the fine mist that looks like smoke. Huge, filament mosquitoes alight on our arms and we brush at them and stare at the other families gathered in groups. Everyone is wearing bathers. Even the fat men and women with pocked thighs and dimpled upper arms.

Our parents help us out of our clothes and into our togs while we have eyes only for the other people. Our mother tells us about lunch and ants' nests and citronella oil against mosquitoes. Though we hear her shouting, we listen only to the tumult of the water. After twenty minutes, we're acclimatised and have eaten. We venture forth to the water that slips and burbles over a multitude of stones, worn silky and smooth by time. Sticks float by now and then, hesitating between pebbles and then continuing. Sometimes a white paper boat with a mitred sail and a soggy hull bobs by. We sit on huge wet boulders near the spray of Curtis Falls. Our mother tells us about her friend's daughter who died of a spider's bite and about another child who wanted to see how long she could control her bladder. After twenty-six hours she was found dead on the timber floor of the earth closet, by her sister. Our mother pitches her voice to a yell, but we still miss the details of some of her macabre anecdotes. She leans over to repeat something and her breath is hot and moist and parts the hair over my ear.

We sit transfixed with fright about the spider, convinced that a nest of redbacks is nearby. I move closer to the spray, hoping that any insects will be washed away before they reach me. Our father tells us that some people in eastern countries sit behind waterfalls for long periods because the air there is healthy. I stare at him waiting for him to laugh because he's made a joke. But he doesn't. I look at my sister. She seems to understand much of what she hears. Her early tantrums have given way to a sort of anxiety. If she doesn't comprehend our parents' conversation, she pretends that she has. I have other ways of covering my deficiencies. At home, in Auchenflower one Sunday, I sat for hours on the hot verandah boards staring at the pages of a book I'd chosen from my father's study. It was titled *The Principles of Electricity* and had elaborate diagrams showing cross-sections of machinery and a thing called a Faraday Wheel. My father finally noticed. He smiled as he passed by with the wheelbarrow:

'Improving your mind?'

I returned the book to its space on the shelf.

My nostrils smart from the citronella and, as my parents talk of other things, I watch the waterfall. In rock pools quite distant from their source, the extremities of spray hit the quiet waters in little, fleeting double U's, reminding me of the rain on our neighbour's iron roof in Auchenflower.

In the mid-afternoon, my mother rubs our shoulders again with Tanafax jelly and we follow the course of the river downstream from the falls. The water is amber in places where it's shallow and ripples over fallen shards of bark. Where it's deeper, it's the colour of sarsaparilla and the stones the other children throw as they play ducks and drakes, sink with a plop. They leave concentric rings which ebb imperceptibly. It's impossible to see where the last vanishes and once again becomes part of the smoothness of the stream. My sister teeters on a log which rests from bank to bank. With her arms out straight and looking like a 'T', she calls as she wobbles:

'Look everyone! I'm in an extremely precarious situation – if I fall in, I have to forfeit my pudding tonight – or have a whole decade of bad luck.'

We watch her.

'You absurd child!' laughs my mother.

My father picks a spray of leaves to swish the mosquitoes. He looks up:

'Girls who swallow dictionaries are so heavy and of such ungainly proportions that they usually *do* fall in!'

She makes it to the other side and runs, screaming triumphantly up the muddy bank, her freesia-coloured hair flying out behind her and her long legs scrambling for a foothold in the slippery undergrowth.

My parents tread the narrow path along the water's edge. Steamy sunlight, diffused from so far above, strangely softens the contours of their faces. The top layer of my father's hair is almost luminous in its paleness. Where the light strikes bleached tree trunks, it casts a glow so their features are lit from underneath. My brother's baby chin is soft as chamois. I could try – but I feel I could never capture, with my pastels at home, the sense of what I've just seen. A man with black bathers almost to the knee and a large straw hat walks toward us. He carefully steps aside to let us pass. His sunburned face creases in a smile:

'Warm enough for yer?'

My father pauses on the track:

'Too right,' and they look into each others faces with the sudden intimacy of the holidaymaker. Encouraged, the man continues:

'A bit close, if you ask me,' and wants to linger.

My mother, further up the track now, mutters:

'Close! – it's *miles* away – what silly things people do say.'

I look back and see my father laugh, showing gaps in his teeth in some places. He touches the stranger's arm rather stiffly, before moving on to join us.

We collect mementoes of Tamborine to press between the pages of *Punch*. My mother has heavy, blood-red, bound volumes of the magazine in Auchenflower. They go back to 1880. Disraeli, his head huge and his body England-shaped, prances a jig. A toe-peeper tramp stretches out the linings of his pockets between finger and thumb. The pages of *Punch* are choked. There are flattened snap-dragons and cross-faced pansies from the chicken-pox epidemic. Squashed two-dimensional mosquitoes from measle-summer and an assembly of four-leaved clovers. We find leaf skeletons, nostalgic and as fragile-looking as gossamer, at Curtis Falls. But touch them, and you find strength and an unexpected harshness in their outlines and the spidery veins within. They travel home to Auchenflower in chapter fifteen of Gibbon's *Decline and Fall.*

We have a short stopover for afternoon tea on the bus trip back. You walk over soft grass strewn with mountain daisies until you reach a large, octagonal cabin. Its name is burnt with a hot poker on a board outside: 'The Gumnut Coffee Hut'. A mass of magenta geraniums climbs and twists to obscure the post the notice is nailed to. Inside it's dark and smells of hot fuel-stove and insect spray. The tables seat four, so my brother sits on my mother's lap. He's tired after a long day and picks petulantly at the wallpaper while we wait. Two piggy-backed flies leave their roost in the sugar bowl.

The waitress arrives and looks with curiosity at my mother who shouts our order above the scraping of chairs nearby. She licks her pencil as she writes and her eyes dart around the room as my mother pauses to choose. The milk jug has a crocheted cover with a heavy beaded border. Our plates are adorned with flat-looking garlands of orange flowers with green leaves and touches of blue. Each table has a tiny vase of blooms like the ones we stepped through before. We eat scones and tasteless melon and lemon jam. My mother says although the tea is weak, it's just as well, as it's all made of Condy's crystals since rationing. She lights her De Reszke cigarette and the smoke curls with lightning speed up her nostrils and comes out like a dragon. While our parents sit and talk over their last cup of tea, we play outside. A tall boy with ginger freckles that almost melt together, takes me behind the Gumnut Coffee Hut. He says there's a box of chocolates there. He gives me a Chinese burn because I won't lift my dress up.

On the bus my mother rummages through her handbag. I hear the squeak of tight cellophane as she untwists the paper round an indigestion tablet. My heart sinks. It's funny how for years you think she's going to produce a sweet when somehow you know it will be a Rennie. I suppose your head knows but your mouth still hopes.

At Callaghan's cottage that evening my mother makes bread and milk and sprinkles it with sugar and nutmeg. Despite the sweetness you can still taste the salt in the bread if you concentrate. We sit and draw waterfalls with pastels on grey blotting paper. My sister shows herself walking on a tight-rope across the top of the falls. My little brother, crouched on the carpet, makes hasty blue streaks for the falls, then a carefully drawn soldier in camouflage lying nearby, rifle at the ready. A Messerschmitt with a back-to-front swastika hovers over the waterfall. The bomb below it hurtles toward the bus he's drawn in the background. Later, in bed we feel the sheets prickle on our sunburned legs. Dark images of the schooldays soon to come, intrude and weave through my dreams that night.

On the last morning, I walk to where the mountain slopes quickly away on one side. When you look down below across the patchworked distance, you can see, in places, the soft suspended floss of clouds where it's raining. And as they move, so their shadows move below in unison. Before we leave Callaghan's cottage my sister and I collect a matchbox each of things to remind us. Hers contains the tightly folded chart of days, some grasses from the side of the house, and the papery corpse of a moth from the bathroom window-sill. My souvenirs include a teaspoon of russet soil from under the house, a splinter of wood from the seat of the swing, and a smooth, thick chip of pale green glass with a bubble in it, that I found in the back of the kitchen drawer.

The journey home is short as return trips always are. We pass the miniature deserted schoolhouse with its tyre swing and white flagpole. And the Hotel St Bernard where the bus hovers idling, to receive the stream of passengers. A magpie stands on the railing of the little red bandstand against a backdrop of clear mountain sky. We move on finally. Cottages, sheds and outhouses thin out to be replaced by the boundaries of forests. You can look deep into their darkness and wonder, if you stepped off the paths and tracks, if you would tread where no one else had ever been. As we continue homeward, the driver selects a low whining gear that provides both a brake for our descent and a threnody for the passing of our stay.

7
AT SANDGATE

It's the summer holidays. 1944. I'm eight – almost nine. My sister is ten and a half and my brothers are twelve and five. Our mother says to watch the sunsets. If it looks like a fine day coming, we'll go to Sandgate. On such a night, my sister and I lie and listen to the wind sucking and releasing the blind and the flying foxes moving restlessly in the figtree outside. Searchlights scan the skies. We watch their long beams flick over the ceiling of our bedroom. In the mornings you can see little patches of dawn sky between the branches of the custard-apple trees. This is the direction our weather for the day comes from. We'll know if the two hour journey to the sea is worthwhile by scrutinising the horizon.

> *Red sky at night is the shepherds' delight,*
> *Red sky in the morning is the sailors' warning.*

When the distance is rosy in the mornings with streaks of charcoal cloud, my sister and I look at each other with despair and flop back onto our pillows. Our mother comes in:

'Now don't fuss – they forecast rain this morning but there'll be plenty of other days.'

She doesn't know that it just *has* to be today:

'My goodness – not tears! You can see that there's not even enough blue sky to make the cat a pair of pyjamas.'

But one morning we're awake before the shadows have time to lengthen across the lawn. The feather-fall silence tells us our mother isn't even up yet. It must be before five-thirty.

Our older brother is back from the 'boarding school' for the holidays. The fact that he's coming to Sandgate this summer adds the final euphoric dimension. We look through branches and see far off so unsullied a sky that we sit bolt upright, then scramble forward in our beds. The cats on our counterpanes, uncoil and their eyes open a little to show milky curtains. My sister reaches through the window with her forked twig and drags forward a branch heavy with sticky mangoes. She selects the one with an apricot-coloured cheek and proceeds to peel it with the knife she keeps in her bed-side drawer. The roof ticks now as the sun climbs higher and there's the plop of a custard-apple on damp grass.

At breakfast the sun slants across the table. A dish of marmalade shimmers, casting an amber spot on the cloth. My father is reading to my mother. She listens, distracted by the ritualistic activities around her, but with great interest. One of the cats stretches up, feather-bellied, to sniff two nectarines that ripen on the windowsill. The tips of its tufted ears are almost transparent. My mother breaks off a piece of toast and butters it:

'Who will you be talking to?'

'It's a speech to the New Education Fellowship – would you children shut up for a minute – how does this sound – "I want to see a world in which economic exploitation and our countless social ills have come to be regarded as we now regard cannibalism." He hesitates. 'Is cannibalism too strong?'

He stops and looks up at my mother. She finishes her mouthful:

'I don't think so . . . but what about "a world in which economic exploitation – was it? – *war* and the rest of our social ills etcetera" – otherwise I like it.'

My parents are always talking about the war. We live in a War Savings Street. It's printed on a tin sign on the lamp post. I can't imagine Auchenflower without the war. A soldier could be dying this very minute. I remember we went to the Regent last year to see *Fantasia*. During the newsreel my mother suddenly sat forward in her seat. The theatre was dark, but light flickered over her face:

'That's my cousin, Tremayne, lying there,' she had said.

My sister and I looked at the screen and saw bandaged

soldiers, arms round each others' necks as they supported the ones who couldn't walk. In mud that looked like thick pea soup, one man lay – not moving at all, his digger's hat shiny with rain, lying near him. Then the camera swung upward to show low-flying aircraft. My mother didn't talk coming home on the tram that day but just stared out of the window.

Now she wipes my little brother's chin with her table napkin and when there's a gap in the conversation I ask if the war will last forever. She puts her cup down:

'I dare say it will end soon,' and looks at my father.

'Will there be any newspapers or seven o'clock news then?' I ask, 'or just music and a long Wilfred Thomas Show at night?'

I started another poem about the war last Thursday. While my mother makes lunch for Sandgate, I sit on the steep back steps to finish it. I want to include all the countries I've heard my parents talking about but I can't find a rhyme for Balkans. I finish and stand near my mother till she wipes her hands on her apron. A tiny green tomato seed clings to the back of her hand and there's another on the edge of the table. She looks at my poem then calls my father to read it to him:

> *'Turned from our loved ones*
> *Turned from our gates.*
> *Germans, Japs, Italians*
> *Sad to relate.*
> *Many towns they conquer*
> *Bombs fall wild and free*
> *And still I always roam*
> *From my native home.*
> *Try to find a place*
> *That's not in enemy hands.*
> *We will never face*
> *All these conquered lands.'*

My sister appears from her bedroom next to the kitchen:

'It doesn't *rhyme* – at least – it doesn't sort of *sound* right.'

My mother pins it on the wall with our drawings and some rows of spidery pot hooks from my brother who's in the Bubs at school:

'It doesn't quite scan, that's all.'

We smell the sea a mile before the train stops at a station near the beach wall. The water is ultramarine as the sun's behind a cloud. Sand banks stripe out toward the horizon and dead transparent jelly-fish litter the shallows. There are dark, jutting rocks far away on our left where the beach seems to turn a corner.

My mother has knitted us brightly coloured bathers. She chose the vivid hues deliberately so that we'd be conspicuous and she wouldn't lose us. It's strange that she frequently threatens to burn down the house while we're asleep, because we're such a nuisance. Yet she knitted us togs that are so bright we feel like clowns. Mine are emerald green with a yellow yacht knitted into the bib. One day I'd like some navy Speedos like the kids at school have. My little brother wears a fawn shirt with tiny, red motor boats on it. Between the craft are printed the words PUT-PUT-PUT in wavy lines.

My mother wades out past the farthest sandbank and lifts him up to sit in a small boat that's anchored there. I follow her, fearful of the water but more alarmed by the two dogs that growl and gambol together, scattering sand, back on the beach. My mother strikes out with grace and strength toward the horizon. Everything she does is definite and unhesitating. She doesn't look back. Not once. I watch my little brother making engine noises and pretending to steer. Reflected shadows of the waves ripple and dance with incredible brightness on the underside of the boat. Since shadows are usually dark, these are like a negative image and incandescent.

I turn to see that my tall brother is pushing a piece of driftwood into the sand. He leans on it, wiggling and manoeuvring until it stands almost straight. He looks around for the balding tennis ball that bounces so well on wet sand. An empty fruit box he finds behind a tussock of grass nearby, serves as a wicket.

Some children from other families come shyly to stand and watch. As they tread on the shining sand, their feet create little dry spots that moisten again in their wake. My big brother looks out apprehensively to sea every few minutes in case my mother should return. The children standing now in a small knot, agree on the boundaries. They point out a sandbar, a tree bent low by years of wind and a slimy sewerage pipe that protrudes from the sea wall.

My mother sits reading now. A floppy straw hat casts a mellowing shade over her brown face. Her legs are bent and she rests her book on her thighs. My little brother stands near her, watching the children. One arm shades his eyes. His knees are thrust back. A toddler squats at the water's edge. He fills a small bucket with water and tips it over his head. I dig a hole which fills continually at the bottom with water. England is down there if I go far enough. I've gathered shells and seaweed pods to decorate the castle I'll make with the growing mounds of sand beside me. My big brother has estimated the size of the children who stand around him. He paces out a short pitch, moving the fruit box forward. Finally the game begins. The children's voices are clear and high pitched. Their beach cries hang in the air momentarily then stop short. My big brother is first batsman and the ball clacks on the whittled fence paling he uses as his bat. My sister bowls, to the unspoken disgust of the boys who stand waiting for their turn. A pecking order will quickly be established through the subtle assessment, by word and movement, of the very young.

A tiny boy stands as fielder, hands on hips, in the shallows. His blue shirt flaps in the wind and the undercurrent drags back against his ankles as he braces his thin legs. His grey shorts are wet as far as the buttoned fly. The game is protracted because a red setter keeps retrieving the ball and racing up the beach with it. The kids are annoyed but they laugh and run after him, wresting the foamy, slippery ball from his jaws. After an hour, the biggest of the other children calls:

'You're in too long, you,' and moves forward.

My big brother, who's had two goes at batting, looks at him for a moment then with a faint smile puts down his paling. A balding man with bifocals and a black singlet suddenly swaggers down to join in. He's been drinking beer with his friends on the hill nearby. His stomach hangs in festoons over his long brown shorts. In his attempt to run-out, the ball hits the fruit box and topples it over with a clatter, smashing the light timber. The children squeal and someone from high up on the dry sand shouts:

'Good on yer, Harry – you show the kids you might be bloody sixty but yer not bloody out.'

The children look forlornly at the remains of their makeshift wicket. A white-haired man leaves the damp towel where he's been lying watching, propped on one elbow. He brings a small wooden chair as a replacement. I sit back on my heels. The hole I've dug is up to my neck. I watch the old man approach the group of children. Tension is in the air. He bends down to a specific child and says something softly. Then he goes to another and standing behind him, swings the home-made bat with his hands over those of the child. Then he takes it himself and smiling, awaits the ball. His glasses glint in the sun and his gaunt legs are slightly bent. There are branches of veins of quite startling blue on his white arms and shoulders. He's bowled out after two deliveries. The children stand back and call out:

'Go on Grandpop – that didn't count – stay there.'

The game is over when the tennis ball is swallowed by the sea and doesn't return.

After our sandwiches my mother takes us over the scorching road to a low-ceilinged tea-room. We buy Two-in-Ones and a packet of De Reszke cigarettes for my mother. The wind from a huge propeller fan overhead plays around our faces as we peel the paper from our icecreams. There are many empty tables and chairs and a faded poster of Mickey Rooney and Judy Garland in *Babes on Broadway*. By the time we reach our towels and buckets, chocolate is running down my little brother's wrists to his elbows.

My mother suggests a walk to digest our food before a final

swim. We pass a row of small, pastel-painted changing boxes to find, further up the beach, rock-pools filled with hot salt water. In some, you see darting fish so tiny and silver you have to blink to make sure they're real. Seaweed tresses are pushed and pulled by the will of the water. I watch their olive darkness and envy them somehow their acquiescence and absence of choice.

The sand squeaks underfoot in places as we continue to walk and the sky overhead is Reckitts blue. My mother, who walks ahead of me, is explaining to my big brother how the word 'horizontal' comes from horizon. With a sweeping motion, she points out to sea. He shuffles beside her and looks up reluctantly then back to his sandshoes. I think he wanted the cricket to last all day. He turns to look back and the sun behind his curly hair, creates an aureole. I hurry to catch up. My mother strides forward. She's bound for a small ornate pavilion we can see far away. It's painted wood and looks like a double-sided bus shelter. It stands in sand half-way between the bluestone promenade and the sea. You can sit facing either the road or the ocean. Victorian spires on either end stand against the sky. The side that breasts the winds off the sea is flaking to reveal silvery grey timber. The roof too is made of wood and instead of its verandah finishing straight across, there's a small overhang of boards cut in U's like the ends of our Two-in-One sticks. Like a timber frill. People have scratched their names all over the pavilion.

> *'Ned loves Dorothy'*
> *'Charlie was here'* and under it,
> *'So was Mary.'*

The earliest date we can find is 1887. My brother notices that on one end, children have drawn a wicket with chalk. A piece of newspaper with a headline reading,'Three Weeks Holds Burma's Fate' has smacked up against the side of the shelter under the seat. It's caught there as if glued, its edges flapping in the wind. My mother turns to retrace our steps. On the way we run down a pier blistered with barnacles. There are sea-baths attached. They used to be segregated, according to an old sign. When you put a penny in the telescope at the end, all you can see is a blur of pale green.

On the way back I find, half-buried, a fat speckled shell. Its edge curls inward. My mother says that if I listen I'll hear inside it the sounds of the ocean. I lift my hair and press the coolness of the shell against my ear. It whispers and reverberates in an orchestration of rushing echoes. How could it register the rumble of the ocean and the soughing of the wind – and yet amazingly it does. I suppose the mystery might be linked with our wind-up gramophone at home in which, somehow, long-ago sounds of voices and music are captured forever.

I watch the houses we pass on the way home. First we travel through seaside suburbs past iron-roofed weatherboard cottages badly in need of paint. Most of the fathers are at the war so fences lean and windows stay broken. Later, a tram takes us through the city of Brisbane and I see the university where my father teaches. He was in trouble last year because he started to wear sandals and shorts on hot days. The people in charge were outraged by this defiance of tradition and banned him from the premises. But few students turned up to lectures and those that did wore sandals and shorts. My father was reinstated after a few days. Our mother points out the building where he started the Workers' Educational Association.

Brisbane city is noisy and dirty. The buildings are graceful and old. Many have generous verandahs and intricate iron lace. There are little spots where shoppers can rest on lawns studded with palm trees. Fountains play and water spurts through lions' mouths for children to cup their hands and drink. There are few cars and those that weave through Brisbane's streets have charcoal burners and gas producers attached. I think it's because our troops need all the petrol.

I often watch the trains that pass through the railway gates in Brisbane. To see metal scroll-work above a doorway or a curved cow-catcher where it could have been straight, seems to indicate that a person has intervened in its manufacture. In a world that's so often utilitarian I find myself looking for such signs. It reminds me that someone helped to make the train, not just a machine in a factory. But in the suburbs on the way to Auchenflower the high-perched timber houses interest me most. When you look down the side of each one, you see miniature tin verandah roofs jutting to shade the windows. Many have their own individual, ornate designs in the supports that attach to the wall. Sometimes there will be a scalloped metal trimming – others have fretwork in complicated shapes and patterns. There's one with a kangaroo carved into it among the curlicues. From the brewery comes the savoury-sweet smell of hops. We must be near Milton. We pass a stand of poplars that, in the wind, turn the silvery backs of their leaves in seeming accord.

At home my sister rushes to the bathroom to wash off the seawater. She can't bear the feeling on her skin. But I won't wash until I have to. Tomorrow I want to lick my arm and taste Sandgate. My father has completed his talk and, over a dinner of riced potatoes, turnip tops and tinned steak and kidney, he reads:

'Fundamentally, I suggest, it is this sort of social change that the present war is all about. I fought in the last "war to end war", and I don't want my son, aged five (my little brother suddenly looks up at him) to grow up just ready for the next one. There must be widespread understanding to help us root out the causes of war. This may involve a new social order in which majority welfare is paramount over minority interests.'

I try to listen but my mind is back at the seaside. I hold my nose to eat the acrid turnip tops. I remember the systole and diastole – the heartbeat of the ocean. And its echo in the lacy half-bubbles that wash and scallop the shore at Sandgate. The sound of the sea is still in my ears.

8
WAR'S END

Today is August the sixteenth 1945. A very important day. I'm waiting for my mother and sister to come and take me home. I've had a lunch of soup and icecream and I'm sitting up in bed in the Sylvia Moffat ward of the Brisbane Children's Hospital. The nurses have attached, with sticking plaster, the front page of the *Courier Mail* to the steel rungs of my bed-head. I keep turning round to look. I used to think when I was little that the war would last forever. But here's the proof that at last it's really at an end. Peace. Those magical letters take up almost all of the sheet of newsprint. I'm ten and a half years old and the war is finally over. It started when I was four. My sister and I quarrel sometimes for two or three hours, then it's finished and we've made up. How could grown-ups argue and fight for six whole years?

Radios play everywhere. I can hear loud ones in the doctors' offices nearby and far away ones over the lawns and garden-beds in the other wings of the hospital. On one station there's no talking at all – no 'Dad and Dave' or 'Martin's Corner' – just party noises and music and Vera Lynn singing her songs. Outside in the streets there are sounds I haven't heard before in my twelve days here. Now and then I can taste metallic blood in my throat from where the tonsils were. Especially when I laugh or call out. Like last night when the nurses were screaming together and dancing round the ward and some of the kids in their striped pyjamas started throwing steamed fish and potato at them. Then the staff carried our cots and beds out onto the verandah. We saw rockets and fireworks soaring off into the night sky and streaming down in a shower of bursting pink and yellow stars, like celestial fountains. I hope my father's celebrating too, down in Canberra. He's been there for such a long time, trying to find a house to rent. He writes every week. He tells us about his job at the university college and how difficult it is to house-hunt and keep up his work too. We hear how lonely and sad he is without us. My poor father. I can't bear to think of him all alone. I wonder if he still has the special times when he dresses in funny clothes and laughs so much. I don't suppose he would without us there to watch. I write to him whenever I can and he always answers immediately.

On the way home, the tram to the city, decked with coloured ribbons and Australian flags, travels slowly. We have to walk through town to the one that will take us to Auchenflower. A fat drunk man kisses my mother as we pass. An airman embraces a sailor. Car horns sound, discordant in their variety. Hats soar into the sky, twirling high above us. Soldiers and civilians drive slowly, in jeeps and cars with gas-producers, through the crowds. Others ride cheering on the running-boards. Party whistles furl and unfurl and shriek their triumph. Toilet rolls drop like curving white ribbons, from the tops of tall buildings. Radios play continuous broadcasts of victory – the announcers shouting like school boys. Girls in their shoulder-padded dresses frolic with sailors and jitterbug in Queen Street. Men with gladstone bags spill out of Lennon's Hotel. I clutch my mother's arm, holding my doll in the other.

The streets are a maelstrom. A small boy sits on his father's shoulders holding high a cardboard sheet. Crudely printed on it is the word VICTORY. I see a young man clamber up an old cast-iron lamp-post to grasp gingerly the glass shade. He holds tight with clenched legs, monkey-like, to the pole. A man in a wide-brimmed Akubra brandishes a half-empty beer bottle. Teenage girls kiss policemen who then join them in their clumsy attempts at the Charleston. I feel confetti tickle my face as it falls. I notice that no shops are open. Even McWhirters is closed today. American sailors throw white caps which hover in the sky like coin spots. Streamers burst from people's hands and ringlet out among those around them.

My sister's shoulders are a mass of pink paper ribbons. One

young woman flings her arms around a constable and embraces him with such fervour that he's knocked to the ground. She lies on top of him shrieking with laughter and his cap falls off and is trampled by the crowd. No one cares, least of all the constable. Red lipstick in the shape of cupid's bows covers his face. Crocodile lines of people conga unrestrainedly down Roma Street past the station. My mother grasps our hands as though we're tiny children. She smiles all the time as she looks around her and we jostle among the crowds; and sometimes she too, returns a kiss. But she doesn't join in. She's too anxious to get us home safely. People pour into churches we pass, to give their prayers of thanks. The doorways are thronged with those who wait their turn. Though it could seem incongruous with the scenes before us, life has a transparency, a vulnerability today.

9
CANBERRA

Sometimes in the soft country evenings the air in Turner smells of the low hedges that surround each house. Kerosene fumes from a primus in a nearby street hang outside my bedroom window. I feel then the frail mood of homesickness for Auchenflower. But so much is a novelty in Canberra there's little room for regret or remembrance.

There are changes in the stories we tell each other at night too. A week ago our mother silently handed my sister an advertisement for sanitary napkins from the *Women's Weekly*. I watched and listened. My mother spoke without turning from her dishwashing:

'There's a flow of blood every month – it happens to teenagers and women.'

We perused the clipping. Table napkins? For nose bleeds? The advertisement was couched in delicate terms that hinted at the embarrassment people feel with these monthly occurrences. Our mother's rigid back as she finished the dishes, discouraged any question or discussion. We looked at each other and fled, our faces suffused with stifled laughter. Our stories are injected now with fresh vigour inspired by the mystery and revelation of that afternoon. Adults, mostly our female teachers, play a larger role than before. Gone are the ethereal princesses who rode on white horses through tangled woods. Our dramas take place either in the staff-room at Canberra High School or the houses we invent for the teachers to live in. We play out our anxieties as each night grows darker, talking at first in whispers then, after our parents retire to bed, in bursts of imagined dialogue:

'Would you like a Modess or a Med?' enquires the protagonist politely in the crowded staff-room, as though offering the choice of tea or coffee.

We invent situations in which teachers in mid-lesson flee their classroom suddenly for the nearest chemist. They emerge, bags crammed to overflowing with sanitary napkins, which they clap to their noses with feverish haste. My sister makes a best friend at school and the stories change. I miss the frenzied and obsessive purchase of napkins:

'What about Miss Prescott passing Mrs Lowe a Modess in the pages of her bible in church?' I interject one night when there's a pause in my sister's latest narrative. She yawns:

'No, stupid. Mrs Lowe's too old for napkins.'

From that time the epics get shorter then stop altogether.

Some weeks after our arrival in Canberra, my sister and I wake to hear our parents' voices raised as though someone has arrived to visit. Pale sun fills the bedroom softly in the particular way of the very early morning. We find our parents huddled together in pyjamas holding the pages of the *Canberra Times*. There are double-page pictures of people standing and lying strangely. They are the skinniest we've ever seen. Their shoulders are like white china doorknobs and their thighs are bowed. They have no hair. Darkness surrounds their eyes and no one is smiling for the camera. They stand near wire fences. Some pictures show towers of bones, in trenches like the one in our back garden in Auchenflower – but long and filling the photo to dwindling perspective. As we peep over our parents' elbows they shut the pages of the newspaper quickly. But I can't dismiss what I've seen. I bunch up a handful of nightie next to my knee and look up at my parents' grave faces:

'Who *are* those people?'

My mother looks for a moment at my father, waiting for him to speak. He's still staring at the closed newspaper which lies at an angle on the sofa. She puts her hands on our backs to shepherd us from the room:

'They're Polish people, darlings. The war was much worse for them than it was for us.'

In the holidays even the early mornings are hot in Turner. My mother gardens at eight to catch the occasional breath of wind. She mutters and swears as she tugs at the spreading couch grass. She finds the transition from Auchenflower difficult.

I escape as often as I can, discovering the many roads that lead to the shops. Most are merely widened tracks skirting the paddocks, but others are asphalted with white kerbing and magnificent in their contrast. I bump and jolt as I ride over hard earth pathways. Narrow and bicycle rutted, their weeds are kept to a minimum by the women who walk miles every Friday for provisions, and for dress materials brought by train from Sydney. But Canberra's roads and tracks aren't busy. I can ride from Turner at the foot of Black Mountain with my green fly veil streaming out behind and not meet a soul. Or walk for an hour looking for lizards along the edge of the pine forest and see no one.

Most of the houses in Turner are new. But there are a few older ones like ours – white stucco with market-garden sized back yards. Ripening pumpkins nestle in grass. And the sappy curling stalks that feed them, wend and weave among flowers that bud and flourish in a matter of days. People know each other in Canberra because it's so much smaller than Brisbane. I can wave as I ride, to the women who stand each morning at their letter-boxes in butterfly curlers and aprons. Just looking. But among the older houses are new dwellings of double-fronted brick. Some are recently completed. Candlewick bedspreads are pinned taut across the bedroom windows. Next door a timber skeleton waits to be fleshed in pale green plaster and finally pink or cream bricks.

In our first Canberra December, summer shimmers down from an unmarred sky. The heat scorches through our cotton dresses.

Sun glints off the silvery roof of our house and dazzles from the handlebars of our bikes. The garden is too hot, even for our mother. She folds her screen away in the wash house and sits inside. We're used to drinking soft rain from the tank that fed the taps in the bathroom in Auchenflower, and Canberra's water tastes peculiar in comparison. On the hottest days it takes two and a half minutes to run cold. My little brother timed it with the watch he got for his eighth birthday. The locals tell us we'll catch the Canberra Wog from the water. No one can escape it. My mother boils everything we drink, but one by one we succumb to the headaches and vomiting. Her illness is by far the worst. My father stays home from the college. He makes us tiptoe through the darkened house. My brother and I trap ants under gum nuts in the side garden and my sister reads *Anne of Green Gables* on her bed. My big brother has run away from home again. In the evenings we eat vegetables all boiled together which my father heaps on to our plates. The potatoes are crunchy in the centre. My mother tells him from her sickbed how to make caper sauce and the house smells for days of the boiled mutton he let burn. Flushed with his creativity, he even makes a huge loaf of bread to save money. It's in the oven for hours and he keeps opening the door to look. Then he sets it triumphantly on the circular wooden bread board where it steams till we cut it. It's black on top and a most unusual shape. We scream and draw our hands back quickly at the moist heat that exudes from each fresh piece. In the centre of every slice is an area of chewy greyish rubber.

We move from Turner to Acton in the autumn of the following year. My sister is almost fourteen and I am twelve. My brother works on a farm just out of Queanbeyan. My little brother is nine and shoots everyone he sees with his new silver cap pistol. He dashes from behind the pine tree and drops to his belly in the grass. My father winces with each shot as he stands at the fly door watching my brother stalk his imaginary foe:
'Did you have to let him buy that thing?'
My mother wipes the baking dish with a honeycomb cloth:

'He said the boys at school all have one. They tease him about his New Zealand accent. It's the least I felt I could do.'

The peeling weatherboard house we rent stands high on the Acton hill in the huge garden of apple and pear trees. Gums and prunus are there too and stretches of long grass. Below us are the Acton flats: we look down on several acres of dirt and stubble cleared occasionally for a circus or a sports day for one of Canberra's small schools. There's a little fibro pavilion and clumps here and there of blackberry. Beyond in mid-distance you can see parts of the road to Civic. One of its curves and bends is obscured by the roof of the new Institute of Anatomy and by the lombardy poplars that surround it. Sometimes on still, yellow Saturdays, we play cricket on the Acton flats. My little brother's high voice is sharp with tension as the ball clacks back and forth. My sister and I dash in our dirndls up and down the suggestion of pitch. We can see our mother, a dot in the garden so far above. She reads in her deck chair. If we scream loudly enough in unison to a count of three, we are rewarded by an exaggerated wave. Once she even gets up and does a tiny Dervish-like dance because she's in a good mood that day. My father tells us that the flats with the Molonglo winding through, host to countless plover-nested islands, will be filled to make a lake one day. Our cricket pitch, our cubbies and secret pathways, will be flooded. The place amid tumbling blackberry bushes where we secreted the stories of our lives in a shoebox for posterity, will vanish forever.

Winter comes suddenly to Acton. The frost-rimed grass crackles under our tyres as we ride, pixie hooded and Fair Isle mittened, to our schools.

Back home my mother sits darning socks and listening to English parliament on short wave radio. Occasionally she ventures through the cold to our sleepout up the rise of the garden near Acton Road. She takes cups of tea and perhaps some biscuits she's baked. We live half a mile from Parliament House and the Commonwealth Statistician, Mr Carver, rents our bungalow for fifteen shillings a week. With a paucity of good company round 14 Acton Road, Mr Carver provides the sort of stimulation our mother craves since leaving Brisbane. There she had her secret left-wing discussion groups and her Trades Hall days where women met to talk and to drink tea. In the bungalow Mr Carver discusses the economy. My mother sits on one of the boomerang-shaped timber chairs my father makes at weekends – he won an award for them in a design magazine. They talk till it's time for her to put the rabbit stew on. Sometimes she adds mushrooms that we gather from moist gullies as we return from school. Once on the way home, we take a shortcut through the grounds of the university college. My father marks papers in the wintry sun of mid-afternoon. He waves and smiles a little:

'Tell mummy I'll be early today.'

When he arrives home, shortly after us, he takes a chair and sits alone in our grove of camphor laurels. He stares out across the Acton flats to the avenues of poplars near parliament, then over the amethyst hills beyond. Sometimes he comes inside to play from his book of Bach. His ability doesn't quite match his enthusiasm. His large fingers falter over the notes of 'Sheep May Safely Graze' and his eyes flick up and down from the music to the yellow keys.

He concentrates so hard he doesn't seem to notice the tears that drop to his lap. Often he strolls to where Acton Road forks. One half of it dips suddenly to reveal a view of such perfection that he returns elated. He sits in the dark dining room near the small window and waits for dinner. His book rests unread on his lap. One Sunday we accompanied him to share the splendour of the panorama. In the foreground is the slope of the road, flanked by the froth and tumble of plum blossom. Then beyond, an expanse of low-lying emerald grass, cut across occasionally by distant post and rail fences like stitching on a wound. And finally, at the horizon, a mountain range – blue as the Granny Bonnets that grow beneath the kitchen window. In a fold of the hills, as small from here as grains of wheat a flock of sheep grazes.

10
EVENING'S SILENT PURPLE MANTLE

Canberra's morning, in late autumn and silently windless, enchants us. We watch from our little bedroom window, the open fireplace still warm from last night. Each huff of our breath clouds the glass. I have time to draw my initials before it clears. Faraway trees are frosted as though a layer of tissue paper hangs in front of the mid-distance. The countryside closer to our house – the poplars, gums and pine trees – becomes a two-dimensional stage set. Neighbouring shrubs and roof tops where there's no chimney to curl a wraith of lavendar blue and dissipate the mist, are more distinct but softened and pale. My little brother and I rode our bikes early one morning in dressing gowns, balaclavas and mittens to see the magic of our own house distanced and shrouded too. The silence in the rest of the house indicates, I feel with some comfort, that my mother is knitting or reading or perhaps doing the cryptic crossword she sends to Sydney for. This morning while we kneel on my sister's bed beneath the window watching the layered backdrops of Canberra's suburban bush, my sister says slowly:

'Winter's canopy ... enveloped the distant trees ... while nature dripped her miniature cascade of sparkling jewels ... '

Here she breaks off, slides from the bed and donning her dressing gown runs from the room.

I dress and wash myself, staring at the small solemn twelve year old face that looks back at me. So like my mother's, people say. I secretly bought a jar of Kintho freckle-remover last week and although my skin is now ghostly white at least I can bear to look at its unmarred contours. On this Sunday morning I find my mother and sister in the sitting room. The fire smells of late May and last night's chestnuts. Sap from the split pine my mother's stoked it with, pops and explodes. Occasionally the mallee root that forms the seat of the flames shifts with a dull thud. Showers of stinging sparks spill out onto the hearth. Our brindled tom cat who sleeps nearby, spits, then resumes his sleeping. My sister sits at our father's desk in the corner of the room, papers around her and scattered on the floor:

'What about this for the ending?'

My mother stops the crossword to listen:

'Noble in its helplessness, a young silky oak, strangled by a luxuriant creeper, raised its manacled boughs imploringly to the heavens. Soon evening dropped her silent purple mantle – velvet-deep and studded with stars – whilst birdsong faded to a diminuendo.'

My mother claps her hand to her mouth:

'My God!'

She laughs loudly, tossing back her straight dark hair. She catches her breath:

'He'll give you an A plus for that – but how about "Whilst birdsong faded to a diminuendo and a hushed yet *pulsating* silence fell".'

I feel for my sister sometimes. She read her first story to our mother months ago. Her face had been taut with pride but had to change to confused laughter after our mother's reaction of amusement at the 'floweriness' of the prose. Since then my sister has forsaken her love of words for the approval shown to her by our mother and Mr Lampton alike.

I feel sorry for Mr Lampton, my sister's English teacher, even though I know he'll probably never realise the source of inspiration for my sister's prize-winning stories. He reads her stories (he likes to call them prose-poems) to the class. They appear in every edition of the school newspaper – submitted by Mr Lampton on behalf of his treasured pupil. He has never taught such an original, imaginative, fourteen-year-old, he tells my sister again and again. With radiant face he pumps my father's hand at school speech nights. My mother and sister glance at each other and turn away to hide their smiles.

I remember once my mother's histrionic whispering as she pored over a book of poetry in the tiny local library looking for Lamptonese. My sister, who'd been researching adjectives in nature magazines, looked up. My mother mopped her eyes as she tiptoed quickly across to us:

'Listen girls!

> *"Lily pads on limpid pools*
> *A pale moon travels slow*
> *Luminous the cloud banks*
> *That rejoice in evening's glow."*'

11
THE TRIUMPHS OF THE FERRET

My sister's friend, Jenny Peverill, arrives after lunch and they sit for hours in the bedroom whispering together. Sometimes they find a private place in our garden in the treehouse my brother made. Or in the secluded dell my mother has planted with bulbs which will show a carpet of pastel green tips in the months to come. The atmosphere with the girls present at afternoon tea, is charged with tension. Jenny Peverill, who has no brothers, discovered boys last summer while watching a group of pimpled Form 5 youths play tennis at the High School courts. Leonard Reece, who wears glasses and Californian Poppy on his hair, becomes her hero. My sister, mystified but compliant, collaborates in her friend's fantasies half-heartedly until she too is bewitched. They never meet him. They watch him from afar. He remains oblivious to their passion. Their stories about Leonard Reece, which I'm occasionally privileged to share, describe a life of extravagant courage, prowess and self-sacrifice. Reality is a bagatelle – it would hamper their imaginations. They insert his name in the popular songs they hear on the radio which become paeans of praise for Leonard Reece.

We sit and talk in the bus shelter one holiday morning. Our hands are numb in our mittens as a gale whips up and down Acton Road. Leaves like giant cornflakes whirl and gather round our feet. A weeping birch stands next to the bus shelter. Its naked winter branches are needle-slender. They curve from the trunk to rise far above us then to hang quite vertically like permanent rain. Jenny Peverill is the first to speak:

'He could be the youngest medical student in the history of

the university. A car knocks him over while he's rescuing a child who's run onto the road. He can't be too badly hurt – just enough so he loses a lot of blood. The ambulance men arrive and he could lie there with tubes up his nose and gasp out his blood group for the transfusion.'

I watch my sister. She's leaning forward. Her tiger-striped fair hair swings across her cheek as she clutches her friend's arm. She breaks in:

'When he's home he could be on crutches. His friends invite him to watch a doubles match one afternoon.'

I listen as she describes how one of the players injures his elbow in a fall during the game. How Leonard Reece throws his crutches down and grabs his friend's racquet. Despite a heavy limp and his obvious agony, they win the game three sets to love. The injury on the road provides unparalleled stimulation for further episodes in a richly heroic life.

Out of curiosity my father feels compelled to witness this natural phenomenon – this paragon of pubescent perfection. Under cover of the school sports day he strolls, directed by the girls, to the courts. We stay well back. My father opens at random the *Canberra Times* he's bought to hide behind. He observes a medium-sized seventeen year old whose pasty face vies with the brilliant white of his tennis shorts and shirt. Leonard Reece dashes to and fro with his racquet. His oily hair is slicked straight back. Not one strand falls out of place as he bends repeatedly to retrieve the ball and to serve. There are faint comb lines that remain throughout the gruelling match. The girls are swooning nearby as they sit close together pretending to knit. I join my father to get a closer look at the object of their rapture.

My father has christened Leonard Reece 'the Ferret' – because he looks as though he's just risen sleek-haired from a river where he's been catching fish.

While my father shaved one morning, he sang loudly so the girls could hear – to the tune of Tchaikovsky's *Caprice Italienne:*

'I know a ferret

> *Who's full of merit
> I love him.'*

I often overhear them when Jenny Peverill stays the night in our bedroom on a mattress on the floor. I fall asleep with their whispering in my ears and the changing, ballooning shadows of the fire that waver around the wall next to my bed. I listen distracted when I'm trying to write my poems at the kitchen table during the cold weekend afternoons.

Tapestries of the Ferret's life are richly embroidered by them as they sit by the fireplace waiting for the chestnuts to pop, or lie together in the morning sun in the hammock that stretches across the angle of the verandah. In the hammock they polish their Granny Smith apples. Jenny Peverill peels hers and is in paroxysms when she tosses its waxy greenness over her head and it lands in a perfect 'L' shape. According to belief she's destined to marry a man with that initial. My sister instructs me to start playing my recorder again and they continue but I play so softly I can still hear their rapturous fantasy:

> During a music theory lesson in his final school year, Leonard Reece yawns and doodles at his desk. (His scribbles equal Leonardo da Vinci's rough sketches.) His teacher, Miss Craig, stops in mid-sentence and looks toward him: 'If you don't want to listen, Leonard, perhaps you could interest the class in something more to your taste?'
>
> Her sarcasm is wasted. He rises slowly. His face wears an artistic brooding look. He strolls to a shining Steinway that happens to be in the classroom. Lifting his coat at the back with a flourish, he sits down. He massages his fingers at leisure then looks out of the window for a lingering moment. His faultless rendition of Liszt's *La Campagnella* leaves the class openmouthed and Miss Craig weeping into her handkerchief.
>
> Soon after, Tennis Professionals approach him with offers of a full-time career. But he refuses. His piano

teacher, who's in love with him, has told him he belongs on the concert platform; that he must tour Europe in the following spring.

His fellow students wonder why he's absent from medical school. They learn that he's penetrated the inner sanctum of the Politburo in an espionage mission for the Prime Minister. He hurries back to Australia to mediate in an industrial dispute – bringing a new and previously unknown era of peace and tranquillity to the unions and management of industry alike.

These last two achievements on the part of Leonard Reece were my mother's grudging contributions. Though she displays amused disgust at the adventures of the Ferret, sometimes we see her pause in her housework to listen to the current fantasy. She overheard the girls whispering one day when we thought she was engrossed in her book. She looked up with a face that registered some impatience, made her suggestions, then flapped her hand at us:

'Now for goodness sake, let me read in peace! Go outside and get some healthy exercise. All this sitting about yarning – it's a positive *folie a deux*!'

12
THE PARTY DRESS

My sister spends a lot of time in front of the mirror these days. The school social is next Saturday night. She parts her hair on the opposite side, then in the middle. She changes her clothes several times each day too. Sometimes she borrows a jade necklace from our mother, or a pair of coral earrings that lie in the japanned box in our mother's bedroom. I recline on my bed watching and wondering. My sister dabs at her face with pink powder she's bought from Coles in Kingston near Jenny Peverill's place. Our mother passes the bedroom door that my sister's forgotten to shut. She's come from outside, letting in the scents of the garden. She dangles a bunch of muddy carrots with one hand underneath to catch the dirt. A dusting of earth, like cinnamon, covers the army surplus boots she wears. She glances in:

'Not looking in the glass *again* child – you spend your whole *life* these days titivating and bedizening yourself!'

My sister stiffens and her face closes suddenly. She puts down her comb and the little compact of powder, and turns away. It seems that it's alright to be grown up – suddenly – like a batch of scones that are soft white dough at one moment, and minutes later quickly risen, tinged with topaz and fully cooked. It's the intervening years that are the problem. There seems to be something obscene and shameful about the transition - about 'becoming'. I sat in the bath last week and looked straight down at two neat little bumps, just discernible and probably only to me. But I cried as I dried myself. Under my pyjamas that night I wore a bandage round my chest as tight as I could tie it and still have room to breathe.

I know what I'll be wearing to the school social on Saturday. My mother is finishing my outfit. It's the first dance I'll ever have been to. It will be held in the Albert Hall, not far from Parliament and about half an hour's walk up Acton Road till you turn the corner. On the right a bus route highway takes you to the hall. On the left is the avenue of poplars which leads to the new bridge over the Molonglo. I've had a vision in my head for weeks as the dance draws nearer. I see myself stepping from the bus and walking up the path and into the ballroom. I imagine my horror if a boy approaches me across the shiny floor for a dance. And the equal horror of one *not* asking while my classmates titter and nudge each other and look me up and down because I'm the only one sitting. I know why I'd be the one wallflower there that night. It's because of my dress.

My mother sits in a deck chair in the side garden. Her screen is positioned to catch the sun, its back section pressed against the prunus tree. Above us is the harsh blue autumn dome of the sky. I can smell the pine tree nearby. I look down the garden and across the Acton flats. One small patch below is bright with yellow broom and over beyond the cricket pitch and pavilion there's a knot of children who wait their turn in a game of rounders. Occasional snatches of their shouting drift up to our garden. My mother whispers as she counts the stitches for the new mittens:

'Fifteen, sixteen, seventeen – that should do.'

She cocks her head to judge:

'No, perhaps a couple more to be safe – *there.*'

I look up at her brown face with its young lines starting round the eyes. She sees me looking and smiles. A questioning smile – as warm as the sun on her knee when I touch it to thank her. My fingers are clenched in my other hand which rests on the grass. I can't tell her. The dress is so pretty. It's taken her weeks to complete. The background is white knitting with pink and blue stylised snow-crystals in a Fair Isle pattern across the chest and round the shoulders. The colours are repeated on the cuffs and round the bottom of the skirt which comes inches below my knees. White knitted socks almost meet the skirt and the Fair Isle snow crystals form a band around their tops. I was able to stop her knitting a cap to match by saying that it would mess my hair for the social. The other girls are wearing flared viyella to just above the knee with full sleeves and coffee coloured lace at the wrist. Some are allowed to borrow their mothers' stockings for the evening and just a touch of lipstick. I heard them talking and felt sick. I want to tell her how beautiful the dress is. How hard I know she's worked. I'd like her to understand how different I'll feel from all the others. I fantasize that we sit casually together and talk almost as equals. I describe my classmates' outfits. She doesn't knit or sew or read, but gives me her exclusive attention.

But such are the delicate, rigid bonds and balances between my mother and me, formed so very long ago and strengthened by my dependency, love and fear, that the possibility of a dialogue like that is just a chimera. I watch her knit the first row. Pink, blue and white strands fall from her wrists across her serge skirt and cling to the thick darned stockings she wears. She lifts her work to show me. The pattern is just starting to develop:

'Look! The beginning of the snow crystals!'

There's a touching innocence about her that's difficult to describe and I grieve inwardly both for myself and her.

On Saturday evening my sister starts readying herself at six o'clock. I can't swallow my food. I look across the dining table at her shining face. At half past seven she tells me I look nice but she doesn't meet my eyes. To my surprise she even dabs my nose for me with her pink powder.

We walk together in the dark to the end of Acton Road then take the short bus trip to the Albert Hall. There are lights outside and all around it, suffusing the bushes and trees nearby. I think it looks like Hollywood. My legs and feet are suddenly very heavy. We walk up the long path to the stone lions at the step, passing stiff rose bushes in a formal garden. Girls with glossy curled hair flock round the entrance talking and laughing with nervous animation. They twirl around to order showing off their new skirts and laugh self-deprecatingly at their friends' compliments. It's cold enough that their breath comes out in whispers of steam. The boys watch from the sides of their eyes. They press down their scented hair with anxious palms and suck their musk lifesavers. The teachers look different all dressed up as we've never seen them before – some minus their glasses.

Inside, the polished floors yawn ahead of me as I look for someone from my class. Lights thirty feet overhead are bright clusters. They illuminate the elaborate cornices. I can see in an ante-room long tables with white ironed cloths and jugs of soft drink at regular intervals. A group of boys scuffles through the door from outside. One of them is pushed ahead by his guffawing friends and sprawls – sliding across the shiny boards on the seat of his pants. The hall starts to fill gradually. Boys one side, girls the other. They pretend not to look across. One boy whistles softly as a senior student strolls through the door in her mother's high heels. I feel everyone's eyes on my legs and school shoes. I look for the toilets in a panic and can't see them. If I could just go somewhere – anywhere – till the ballroom is full and I'm not so conspicuous. Two of the girls from my year approach me:

'Did your mother make your outfit? It's so pretty.'

They're really trying. But somehow I feel worse – like an object of pity instead of ridicule as I'd expected. As casually as I can manage, I retrace my steps to the front door. Mr Ricks, my science teacher, smiles my way:

'Enjoying yourself?'

I think even *he* is looking me up and down. I barely meet his eyes:

'Yes thank you, but I'm trying to find someone – they might be outside.'

The bus back to Acton Road comes after ten minutes. I walk home slowly to take up time. Mr Carver's light is on in his bungalow. The dog in the house on the other side barks just once when I tread on a stick. There's a rectangle of light on the grass at the kitchen window. I look inside. My father is sitting at the table with his head in his hands. My mother stands near him pouring from the teapot. Her mouth moves and I can hear occasional words. They're talking about the university. As she leaves the room with the tray, the light swings slightly with the movement of her passing and the fridge in the dark corner is momentarily lit by its swaying spill. My father remains there. After some moments his chest heaves in a sigh and he puts his palms on the table, elbows up like a frog, rises slowly and leaves the room.

My mother looks up alarmed when I arrive in the sitting room doorway. Her finger marks her place:

'What on earth are you doing home? It's only just after nine.'

I cross to the fire and stretch my frozen hands out, almost touching the flames:

'Didn't I tell you? They send the first year students home early.'

13
COUSIN BREADCRUMB

Zelda Goldstein, wife of a colleague of my father's, visited us after lunch today. She's one of the few friends my mother has made since our arrival in Canberra three years ago. Zelda Goldstein is what my parents describe as a 'fellow traveller', which has something to do with the Communist Party. I always used to think it was because she picked up my father in her little yellow car each morning to take him part-way to the college, on her trip to the library where she works. Occasionally she eats with us. She sits watching my parents as she eats mushroom pie or pea soup. She laughs a lot, jerking back her head of frizzy black hair at my mother's comments. She says: 'Oh you are awful' so often that my sister and I start counting one evening and get to seven before pudding.

I can hear my mother and her friend talking in the sitting room. Since I've learned to read music properly, conversations sound as though, if they were written down on manuscript paper, they would have little sideways 'v's' above every few words for accents. My mother's usually loud voice is lowered. Their teacups clink in the saucers and they speak in tones that invite closer attention.

I proceed carefully, choosing the boards at the side of the passage to avoid the familiar creaky ones down the middle. Zelda Goldstein's slightly nasal voice is muted like my mother's. She clears her throat before speaking:

'When I think of *Harry*, who's the same age and has so much *go* in him and you *must* worry about things like that strange business in the staffroom – I mean it was so uncharacter*istic* of him.'

At door level now, I wait for my mother's reply:

'It's not so much *that* – after all he *comes* from a family who are *gi*ven to eccentric *out*bursts.'

She stops for a moment:

'You know, he has a cousin who thinks he's a *bread*crumb and spends his *whole* life in*side* to avoid birds.'

Her cup clinks again:

'No, it's more his constant *worry*ing these days and long face about *nothing* – I think he *needs* something – some other interest apart from all the books and lecture writing.'

She pauses and I can hear the crunch of a biscuit. My curiosity about what sort they are and whether there'll be any left for me later, almost prevents me from concentrating as my mother speaks again over her friend's voice which is saying:

'I'm sure there's some way we can help him if we . . . .'

So my mother reiterates:

'It *may* have something to do with that *year* he spent here in Canberra house-hunting before we joined him . . .'

Her voice dwindles for a moment. She must be thinking. Then it continues:

'*You* know – alone for so long – oh, I know he had his *friends* and the Gibsons who cared for him so well. But when we arrived from Brisbane all I can say is that I found him *greatly* changed.'

Their conversation becomes more general and I creep past and into my bedroom to finish the bottle of Passiona with the teat on it that I keep in my bedside drawer. I can see the verandah from here. I read the name 'Lysaght Lysaght Lysaght' across its corrugated underside just like the one in Auchenflower. And I wonder for a moment about the adult world. If you really thought you were a breadcumb I suppose you'd be afraid of dust pans and brushes too. And how dreadful to worry about being put around a lamb cutlet and fried. The sky outside is silver – with the tallest branches of the tree next door pushing up into the billows of gunmetal clouds that are gathering beyond. Even darker ones roll back behind them.

. . . skies of couple-colour . . .

I can hear the blackbirds too that love so much to sit on our wire fences. I remember as I grow colder in the darkening bedroom, my father reading us Hopkins last night after dinner. Words and phrases have been insisting their way into my head ever since.

> *... skies of couple-colour as a brindled cow ...*
> *Finches' wings ... landscape plotted and pieced*

In his chair near the fire, shoes tiptoed and knees together to hold the book, he'd read:

> *'He fathers-forth whose beauty is past change.'*

He'd swallowed then and could read no further. I want my poetry to be as good, but it never will. In the verses last night the words hunched and clung together so you could hardly breathe. There was an essence in them that describes the sort of exhilaration that you sometimes have yourself. An impulse you can't evoke merely by wishing it to happen.

As I lie here watching the chiaroscuro of quicksilver shadows on the wall beside me, the evening brings to life a day several weeks ago when my father sat reading in the darting shadows of the prunus tree. I watched him from the tree-house above and listened as he read some passages from the book on his lap to my mother who sat darning socks opposite him.

You could tell that the book was very important to him. It was the story of a man who goes to see a trick cyclist. I thought at first it must be something to do with a circus. But my father, when I asked later, explained. And I found myself talking with him about the book. I remember being vividly aware that it was the first time I'd ever really talked with my father. I mean just him and me. I'd never realised that you can try to heal a sick mind by talking – just as you can treat a painful part of your body with medicine, or rest, or an operation. My father told me there's an old man in Switzerland called Dr Carl Jung. He's named part of our minds the Collective Unconscious. It means that we're really all joined in some way.

Our minds are divided into sections. There's the part that decides, remembers, and imagines. And another compartment whose contents we don't know. The old doctor calls it the unconscious – here we have tucked away events or feelings that make us do strange things.

When I think of Mrs Cruikshank at number 7 Acton Road, who kisses every flower in her garden and talks to herself, then I realise she's obeying some voice in that part of her mind. And I can more easily accept the breadcrumb cousin too.

I wonder about those times when my father talks and shouts with such excitement and joy – so unlike his usual self – and strides about, reading aloud from his books while we're meant to be asleep; and my mother is confused and angry and tries to make him return to his quiet self.

I reflect on how well I know my body from looking at it, and feeling when it's got a cold or a headache. But it frightens me to contemplate a locked room in my head. Anyway, I don't suppose that, at twelve and a half, I'd have that part yet. Remembering my mother's conversation with Zelda Goldstein, I watch my father at dinner to see if I can notice differences from the picture my memory paints of him in Brisbane when I was ten. But I can't. Well, only one thing. Sometimes when I'm not able to sleep, I hear him walking up and down the passage. Or the verandah if it's a still night and warm enough. He holds a torch. Its beam bends and stretches and sometimes he whistles under his breath, parts of the B Minor Mass. One night I walked to our bedroom door to look and when he saw me, he held the torch under his chin for a moment. Its light bathed the planes of his face and the shadow of his nose flickered upward. He smiled at me and murmured:

'There is a willow grows askant the brook . . . therewith fantastic garlands did she make.'

He passed by, then glanced back over his shoulder:

'Does nature's sweet nurse elude you?'

I knew it was a quotation from somewhere. I suppose my standing there in my nightie reminded him of something.

But the longer I look at my father solemnly cutting his meat in mathematical segments and the more I think about him, the more strongly I feel that I'm coming to a strange conclusion – that he has never really been comfortable being inside himself. He seems at times, when I think back as far as I can remember, to be partly elsewhere. Almost like the effect you see sometimes in a picture where the colour doesn't quite touch the outline of the drawing because it's been printed carelessly. When he reads by the fire you can see him look up from his book at the changing patterns of the flames in the hearth. In the garden, he gazes toward the horizon. Doves that have waited nearby for crumbs, then rise swiftly and wheel away behind him, banking when they strike the up-currents, and the pages of his book peel back and flutter in the wind – while my mother, if she's nearby, just keeps on knitting or shelling peas as if she knows exactly what is right for her. But then I think of how he plays the piano from his Bach book. And at those special times, rides his bike in crazy zigzags across our huge stretch of grass at the side of the house to make us laugh. And the parts of him, then, seem to unite and you can see a whole person. I must have been staring for a long time, engrossed in my thoughts, because I find him looking across at me. I glance away – but not quickly enough:

'I'll give you a penny ha'penny for them this time, they seemed like important ones!'

14
A YOUNG MAN'S FANCY

It rained all last night. Large, tepid spring drops at first. Then a downpour that hammered on the iron roof. This morning my mother and I stretch out the sodden sheets on the line and back away when the wind catches them and they billow like spinnakers. She picks off the gum leaves that have blown into their dripping folds:

'God always knows when I do the washing and punishes me for not believing in him,' she laughs.

The boy who lives in the Acton Guest House up the road, walks down our long gravel drive in his short school pants and blazer. I run inside before he sees me. My sister, aged fifteen, sits finishing her homework. She looks through the dining room window and turns to me:

'Oh, NO – it's the ubiquitous Ian Holden – quickly *hide*!'

But I can't. I'm late as it is. She runs, through the back door out into the wind and eddying leaves, mounts her bike and vanishes down Acton Road toward Canberra High. I sit on the bedroom floor to tie my shoelaces. My mother appears in the doorway:

'Ian wants to know if you'd like a dink to school.'

I feel cornered. Thoughts of pneumonia or a broken ankle or even food-poisoning flit through my mind. But five minutes later I'm a mile down the road on the back of his bike with my legs dangling and aching already. I notice a small pimple that keeps appearing and disappearing into the ribbing on the neck of his jumper as he pedals. I'm nearly thrown off as we jolt over the gutter and into the paddocks that flank the quadrangle of the school. But I don't like holding on round his grey serge waist even though he keeps swivelling his head and saying:

'Go on! Hang on to me – I won't bite you.'

I'm puzzled by his constant requests to accompany me wherever I go. Why has he not asked before? We've lived so close for eighteen months and until now, he's either ignored me or bumped me off my bike at every opportunity.

When we get to know him better, my sister and I play ping-pong with Ian Holden on Saturdays, in the gloom of the cavernous Guest House lounge.

At his fourteenth birthday party we eat Milk Arrowroot biscuits that Ian Holden's mother sticks together with almond icing and arranges on a plate. And scones spread with plum jam. Her dishes have a gold rim and you can see Mrs Holden's crimson thumb-nail reflected as she puts the platters on her card-table.

But sometimes when my sister's not there Ian Holden doesn't like playing ping-pong. He chases me along the Guest House corridors making gorilla noises. When he catches me he tickles my ribs so hard and for so long that it's difficult for me to get my breath. His face, close to mine, smells of peppermint and his armpits of sweat. His mousy hair tickles my nose. He becomes very interested in the clothes I wear. He says he likes my gathered cotton skirt and ask me to twirl round and round in it. He watches closely till I'm giddy and the hem almost touches my outstretched hands.

In the Guest House lounge one afternoon, Ian Holden's mother picks up her tapestry and silken thread and leaves to make a small rabbit pie for herself and her son. He closes the door behind her, places his bat on the ping-pong table and comes to stand alongside me. He puts his hand on the puffed sleeve of my blouse:

'I'll show you if you'll show me.'

Does he mean he'll show me how to improve my backhand? Then what could I possibly show him? He's an expert at table tennis. But something in his manner tells me that what he's said has little to do with ping-pong. I want to run home quickly to where I know my family will be sitting in the safety and status quo of the sitting room. After a moment, in which Ian Holden stutters his confusing truths, I back away from him and look up at his anxious, darkened face:

'But – I don't need to see *that* – I've got two brothers.'

Aware, somewhere inside myself of his need – but not really caring about his curiosity or anything except escaping, I walk quickly to the door and out into the shining afternoon.

He asks the same question at every opportunity and his presence becomes more a threat to me than a pleasure. One Saturday morning I wash my hair and sit in the sun on the small verandah of our sleep-out. A shadow falls across my feet and I look up to see Ian Holden's familiar, tentative smile. He's balancing knuckle-bones that he's gathered from the Acton flats and wants to play a game of jacks. He sits beside me and I notice that pale hairs now coat the bottom half of his legs. He looks over to the fly door which leads inside our house. Then he turns to me:

'Where's your mum and dad?'

'I don't know – I think she's gardening round the front and daddy's just gone down to buy milk.'

Ian Holden breaks in to the end of my reply, pointing to one of the cats that lies nearby:

'Hey, that cat's a girl – look!'

'So what – of course it's a girl.'

'But – I mean – look at its tits.'

I look at its tits.

'Has she had babies?'

'Kittens you mean. She had Gemmy – you know the one with the diamond on its back – remember it got run over – and in the same litter she had Penny who ran away.'

His interest in the cat's progeny is fleeting:

'Yeah?' He pauses. 'You know how she had them?'

'Yes, of course, my sister and I helped her – I mean – we kept everyone away and got a blanket for her and some food when she'd had the last kitten.'

'Yeah, but d'you know how the kittens got *in* there in the first place?'

'Well – '

'You don't, do you – you don't know what *that's* for, do you?'

He points with a long twig, under the cat's tail, to a little fluffy protuberance. I look down at the hard ground where a few blades of new grass thrust upward in tiny bunches. I'm getting a bit sick of Ian Holden today and it's nearly half past ten and my hair's practically dry. But he's relentless this morning, in his desire to impart information. He seems excited and jumps up to crouch opposite me where he can see my face. Or almost – because my hair's covering half of it. I squint across at him but say nothing. In the green part of his eyes, I see reflected, the bungalow window in miniature.

'D'you want a clue? It's to do with the male cat.'

'Well, I know that.'

I want to stop the conversation but something drives me to listen, almost against my will:

'Well – if you know it's to do with the male cat, you must know what happens!'

I'm trying to make sense of what he's saying. I keep squinting at his face. My eyes are watering in the sun.

'I'll give you a clue.'

He half-stands and reaches into his pocket to produce a matchbox. I look briefly at the matchbox then back to his face. His eyes seem riveted to mine and he talks and stammers and tumbles over his words. He pulls out the small, blue cardboard drawer that has a few matches left in it. Then he rapidly pushes it back and forth several times. I feel breathless. He's gone mad. I watch him knowing he hasn't. My mind is in spinning turmoil at the ramifications of what Ian Holden has just so graphically shown me. And then I experience the belated, gentle awakening in my head, like the sort of trigger you have some days, for the memory of last night's dream.

I leave Ian Holden sitting on the edge of the verandah and

walk across the little courtyard formed by the wash house and Mr Carver's bungalow. Smoke from my father's bonfire gusts across the garden. Over the wide stretch of lawn on the other side, is a dense thicket of overgrown jasmine. I push my way in and sink down on to spongy undergrowth. The garden I see before me of smoky trees and berry bushes – with my father's barrow near the triangular stack of pine logs, wavers, distorted for a moment. Then I blink. Part of me is conscious of the deep, blue smell of violets somewhere close by. I have a sour taste in my mouth. Incidents that have happened and conversations that I've heard for years, that have had an incomprehensible element in them, click rapidly into place, just as my mother tells me dying people's lives flash before them. I feel shame that I'm thirteen and I didn't know. I look out from my protective labyrinth of leaves at the new world.

15
BY THE HARBOUR

In the early days of the 1948 summer when I'm thirteen and a half and my sister's fifteen, our mother plans a visit – just for my sister and me – to stay with our legendary aunt who lives in Cremorne on the edge of the harbour in Sydney. During the long train journey, I sit with my back against hard, buttoned leather. My cousin will be eleven now but I can only see her as a black-eyed baby. We pass fields that stretch to the horizon. Square-shaped cows flick their tails to shoo the flies and sheep scatter in a fan shape, running from the noise of the train.

Our mother used to tell us how her sister's beauty had driven young boater-hatted men to distraction when she was an art student several years before her marriage. One persistent admirer had followed her around the entire world. I don't know about my sister but I've always imagined that young man perpetually on his knees, hands clasped before him; in the dining rooms of steam ships that dipped and rolled through white-flecked oceans; on the decks above, as he stared at my aunt in her silk scarf that ballooned in the salt breeze. Or watching with despair as she gazed out to sea with studied inscrutability, well aware of her suitor's omnipresence. I have in my mind a picture of her in a diaphanous dress that swirls to the neat turn of her ankle; of a face with skin of alabaster and mahogany eyes fringed with lashes as dark as pitch – eyes that stare out to sea awaiting creative inspiration. Then I imagine her stooping briefly with effortless brittle comments to her kneeling Romeo as, weeks later, she sweeps through the cobbled streets of Paris or Rome with her light sea chest in one artistic hand (she didn't need many clothes – her beauty was such that she could wear the simplest attire) and her canvases and palette in the other.

I remember how I rushed home from nursery school on the day of her arrival in Auchenflower to visit us for a week when I was four. I saw before me a woman so like my mother, I could only stand and stare. But my mother's face was darker from the Queensland sun. Instead of filmy skirts and fine, pleated blouses with full sleeves, my aunt wore dark slacks and a high necked black jumper. Her straight ebony hair was drawn back with long bobby pins. She was thirty-three years old. She had my mother's charcoal eyebrows. The face beneath was animated and its features perfect. She was holding under one arm a dimpled rolypoly infant, a little older than my younger brother. A baby whose head was a complete sphere with a thicket of black hair. And eyes like buttons, set in a face whose main feature was the salmon-pink rotundity of its cheeks. I remember putting out my arms and the baby, whose name was Cosima, wriggling to come to me. Memories of the things our aunt did on that visit were to remain with my sister and me.

One of them was the fact that when her baby had finished sitting on her potty, my aunt would crumple up the piece of toilet paper, till it was soft and warm, before using it. We noticed also her casual manner toward the infant who was allowed to totter along our verandah to the edge of the steps without being restrained or cautioned. Our mother would jolt forward in her striped deck chair with alarm, while our aunt lounged back with her claret in one elegant hand watching the scene with amusement:

'Let her go – she knows about stairs – we had much steeper ones in London last year. She'll learn better if we don't fuss over her.'

My sister and I pass through outlying suburbs now. We speed through Strathfield. Canberra is 187 miles behind us. Steam from the engine in front bursts in cotton wool gusts and obscures our view, then we look down into the backyards and private lives of the people who live in the railside dwellings. A child leaves an outside toilet through a sawtoothed door and hitches up her pants before running across to a tyre swing. A man tends his garden without even a glance at our clattering train. His wife pegs washing nearby. We stagger for the last time down the narrow corridor to the Ladies, battering involuntarily with our shoulders against the panelled wood that partitions each compartment from the passageway. And we take our last sips from the chained mug which hangs next to the railway-thick glass carafe. Its remaining water lilts with the motion of the train. We consult the pink pages of the Gibney's our parents gave us before we left. 'Sydney and Outlying Suburbs' it says on a squirly ribbon across the front cover. Behind the ribbon, houses and buildings are sketched around the edges of a pencilled harbour and its bridge. My sister looks at me:

'We are about to experience two weeks of unparalleled sophistication and opulence. We must not swear lest we offend the rarefied sensibilities of our gracious hosts and we must conduct ourselves with impeccable manners at all times.'

She takes down our school cases from the wire rack above us and hands me mine. I grasp the metal handle finding great comfort in its familiarity. My whole body is starting to fizz with apprehension:

'But how will we know where things are – like the lavatory?'

'We'll *ask*, stupid.'

She strides ahead with seeming confidence. I feel my own smallness. And my usual admiration for her.

Our mother told us at home that our aunt and uncle's land, though small at the back of the house, stretches out in front and slopes down steeply to the lapping water's edge. But we're not prepared for what we see when we arrive at Kareela Road, Cremorne. The front garden reminds me most of the rain forest at Tamborine in Queensland so many years behind me now but still vivid in my mind. My sister says it's like the Secret Garden. She stands on the verandah that overlooks it at almost treetop height. We can hear the occasional muted slap of water far below between the trunks and foliage of thickly planted red-gums, begonias and agapanthus. Our aunt gathers corn and spinach for the evening meal and we wait for the arrival of our cousin from school and our uncle from his office of architects. The sitting room has double doors that lead onto the high verandah and we turn then and step through. The walls in here are palest olive with a white ceiling. There are soft leather chairs and cream-coloured seagrass on the floor. My sister looks at her wrist:

'At six pm on the eighteenth of November nineteen forty-eight, we entered the portals of paradise.'

The dining room table in one corner of the large room, has chrome chairs in a sort of partial 'S' shape with leather seats and backs. The lights which hang low over the dining-table are huge paper balls which glow softly as the room darkens with the approach of evening. Then our cousin appears in the doorway in her private-school uniform. Her face is almost unchanged in nine years. I look down at my suddenly dowdy skirt. And socks that have gone to sleep in the backs of my school shoes. At least my father polished them for me before we left for the station. The bedrooms are across a passage. Our cousin takes us first into hers. My aunt has borrowed mattresses for us which lie on the floor next to our cousin's bed.

Her room is so full of toys, games and ornaments we don't know where to look first. A doll with a face as sweet as a daisy and long real hair to its waist, sits in a wicker chair beside my cousin's bed. On the window-sill is a row of china pigs, graduated in size and decorated with dark green four-leafed clovers. Under the window there's a small table and on it a richly-detailed miniature theatre, complete with interchangeable backdrops. Real material curtains in ruby-red velvet have tiny golden ropes to tie them back and to release them between the acts. It's set up for *Othello*. There are the gothic archways of Venice. And Desdemona with her swarthy, magnificent bridegroom to her left. The noble Moor stands on his little tab of white cardboard and gestures, one arm outstretched, as he mouths the unheard eloquence of his poetry. We notice with astonishment, pound notes casually lying here and there in our cousin's bedroom. One in a small box of hair ribbons. Another peeping from under a book on our cousin's desk near the window. There's even a five pound note folded up near her money-box. I touch the one in my pocket with anxious fingers – the most money I've ever been given in my life – and hope it will last till I get home.

In the kitchen our aunt prepares a meal of unfamiliar dishes. There's artichoke soup and creamed spinach with butter. Caramelized carrots sprinkled with caraway on a pottery plate in the oven, and meat in large grilled pieces, not cut up and stewed. We smell a new mouth-watering aroma and taste that night garlic sauce and mignonette lettuce. And pancakes with frilled edges. Our aunt passes a jug of brandy and orange sauce around the table. We laugh and refuse when our handsome uncle offers us wine. But we sip a little from his glass instead. After dinner we sit in the leather chairs and our cousin brings out a game called Shove Halfpenny. The adults drink black coffee and Benedictine and our uncle smokes some strangely aromatic cigarettes. But they join our game. When I make a mistake my uncle horsebites my leg just above the knee. And the ice is finally broken for us all.

Later that night before bed, my aunt shows me how to draw a gumtree by scribbling vertical pencil strokes for leaves. She's a satirical artist who works for a glossy Sydney magazine. Once or twice a week she takes her pictures by ferry across the harbour. I look through her studio, touch canvases, jars of turpentine and half-used tubes of paint. She promises to let me try some of her thick textured paper and charcoal sticks in the days to come. My aunt is not demonstrative like my mother and I'm surprised at the lack of ceremony at bedtime. I lie still that night on my alien springy mattress and listen to the strangely different sounds of a Sydney night. I wonder what's happening at fourteen Acton Road.

My aunt's kitchen always smells of fresh coffee in the mornings and a lingering scent of lemon. She has posies of fresh verbena and ranunculus and other multi-coloured flowers in a bowl on the wooden table. Sometimes in the evenings she winds a strand of fragrant jasmine round the base of a candle in the dining room or floats a single camellia. She does these things deftly with a sort of sureness. It reminds me of some aspects of my mother and I think of her back in Acton Road with some sadness. Their similarities and contrasts are a constant source of interest to my sister and me as the days by the harbour unfold.

Our uncle has a jeep with canvas pieces on its sides that flap in the wind as we drive. He lets us sit on the bonnet or cling onto the back as he speeds along the hills in the suburbs on our sightseeing trips. We scream with elation and fear and the louder we shriek, the faster he drives. I'm always relieved when we stop. But I never say I am. Our aunt sits beside him. Sometimes I ride inside. Once she leant over to look at the speedometer and said matter-of-factly:

'I think perhaps sixty is a little foolish with the girls riding on the front.'

So he dropped his speed. She never appears to get angry about anything. She's the most laconic person I've ever met.

She stands in the bedroom doorway one morning while the three of us compose limericks. Each verse is more daring than its predecessor. My sister is hesitating over a rhyme for entrails so my aunt seizes her opportunity:

'Any smalls for the wash? I want to fill the machine.'

I puzzle over the word 'smalls'. Then relief floods over me. I'm down to my last pair which I've already worn once. Thank goodness she asked – I could never have mentioned anything as vulgar – as personal as underwear. My sister and I collect our little bulging washing-bags our mother made for us before we left and empty them into the machine. Our aunt closes the lid and presses the button:

'Why didn't you let *me* put them in, you silly girls – then you needn't have got out of bed.'

But nothing as mundane – as unspeakable as my vests and bloomers should pollute the pristine sophistication of my aunt's hands.

Back in bed, on that lazy morning, I think of my parents in Canberra. While my aunt is pressing buttons, my mother is probably chipping kindling to stoke the copper this very minute. I imagine her stooping in her apron by the stack of pine, her hands busy with the splintery pieces she heaps in her pinny, and her mind elsewhere. I see Mr Carver step from his bungalow verandah and cross to her in the sun, where he stands, hands in trouser pockets because it's Saturday. My father could be reading the *Canberra Times* right now under the plum tree, his pipe resting beside him on the grass. He might look across at my mother for a moment with her apron bunched, then to Mr Carver, and wish she would talk with equal animation to him. My little brother is probably far away on his bike. Or making yet another brown paper kite to float in the sky above the Acton flats. My aunt appears again in the doorway holding a colander of copper onions:

'We thought you might like to eat at Le Coq d'Or tonight – we usually do – and there's probably no equivalent in that quaint little piece of real estate masquerading as the Federal Capital Territory.'

I adore the drollness of her voice and my sister and I look with delight at each other across the bedroom. Both at her vision of our beloved Canberra and at the prospect of going out at night to eat in a restaurant. We look back to our aunt who's saying:

'Oh, and do you fancy a little French onion soup for lunch?'

I wash myself in the luxury of the tiled olive-green bathroom. I'd never had a shower before Sydney. It's always baths at home. Sometimes my mother gets in with me. I have nowhere to look except the ceiling. I think it's her way of showing me how I'll be when I've developed properly but her silence is unnerving and the little dark moth-shape between her legs, disturbs and terrifies me with its omen.

I look that evening, with sadness for my mother, at the dresses she's put in our luggage. One each for special outings. But they're not quite right my sister says, for dining in the grandeur of a night-club in the metropolis. So we cram ourselves into our cousin's skirts and frilled blouses and our aunt lends us some stockings. Át seven o'clock we enter Le Coq d'Or, to be met by a waiter with a bow tie and pleated white shirt. He holds the chairs back for us till we sit, as though we're weak or paralysed. Then fluffs out table napkins to put across our laps. The menu is French which I've started to learn at the high school this year. I can see a dish whose name I think I can decipher:

'Ground apples sound nice,' I say tentatively, making conversation. 'I suppose they mean apple puree.'

My sister nudges me hard, crunches her heel down on my shoe and shakes her head at me frowning. My aunt and uncle smile my way and say they'll order for us all. My face is hot and tight with mortification. Doesn't 'terre' mean ground? And 'pommes' – apples? I won't speak again tonight. We eat plum soup to start. Mine's icy cold so it must have been served in the kitchen long before the others were. My sister looks at me warningly so I know something must be wrong. Perhaps hers is cold too. Then we're each given an omelette – all alone on the plate with a miniature bunch of parsley on top. The omelettes are covered with a transparent glaze of something like marmalade. The vegetables come later on a separate dish. The lights in here are small lamps that glow ruby-red from the darkness of the walls. And there's thick carpet under our feet. And cubes of butter in shallow silver dishes of cold water. My aunt and uncle drink purple wine that the waiter continually darts over to replenish the minute they finish each glass. Having poured, he twists the bottle quickly with rhythmic dexterity and a flick of his wrist, so no drop falls to sully the cloth. Then he replaces it in its bed of ice.

We return to George Street where my uncle's jeep is parked and travel home through the dazzling streets of Sydney's city. There are trams too just like Brisbane. Necklaces of light stretch before us. We leave for the suburbs. Multi-coloured neon signs flare and blink behind to give the silhouettes of far-off theatres and night-clubs a nimbus that reflects in the waters of the harbour. My uncle turns his head to speak to us where we sit in the back seat of the jeep:

'Well, my little country mice, I hope that gastronomic indulgence won't keep you awake tonight.'

I look out at the tall houses. Sometimes a light from a porch winks through the trees as we pass. And I see a child look up from drawing to listen for a moment to the unaccustomed sound of the jeep. Twice, a growling dog scuffles alongside us and barks at the intrusion into his slumber. I feel a sudden flicker of homesickness, then we're coasting, engine off, down Kareela Road toward the house.

My uncle has a huge workshop under the verandah. There are sheets of dull copper and lengths of beautifully grained wood for his many projects. One night after dinner he takes me down there. He measures my wrist and the next morning at breakfast, tells me to shut my eyes. When I open them he has, lying in his hands, two bracelets. One is a thick copper spiral of one and a half twists. He shows me how to rub it with steel wool when it clouds. The other – my initials perfectly carved in wood then strung together on fine elastic so that I can push it over my hand. Each small letter is dark brown with a wavy grain and polished to a dull patina. I hug my film-star uncle so hard he says:

'Hey, steady on,' and puts his pipe down to laugh.

Our uncle takes us on a ferry one night across the harbour to Luna Park. He sits inside the cabin but we watch from the deck, the lights of Sydney and their evanescent reflections. The salt wind whips our hair in all directions. We have eyes only for the distant neon sun-rays of the Fun Park as it appears across the water. Canberra has no such place. We've seen nothing like the glowing wonderland that grows closer as the ferry makes its last turn across the harbour. We're close enough now, that we can hear faint screams on the wind that furrows the dark waters around us. I turn to make sure my uncle knows we're almost there. I notice a spatter of cats-paw rain on the cabin windows and inside my uncle sees me and raises his pipe in acknowledgement that it's time.

We step off the ferry and I look at my sister and cousin. Their faces flash rhythmically with blue light, then pink. We enter the laughing mouth below neon teeth. You can smell vanilla from here. The men who take the visitors' money at the turnstiles don't seem excited at all. One is even reading a *Captain Marvel* magazine and only briefly looks up to count us. Then back to the comic as he hands our uncle the change. The vanilla smell grows stronger and I notice a woman behind a counter, who curls what look like squares of brown lace around a stick as though she's been doing it all her life. And there are checked waffles in a pile on her other side, that she injects with cream. On our right, sailors, who seem to be wearing neck-to-knee bathers, stand behind beach scenes with their head in indents, while flash-lights pop. There's a booth hung with the delicate fuzz of Floss Candy in huge paper cones. But here they call it Fairy Floss. My uncle sees me looking, and minutes later I taste the fleeting sugariness of the confection and feel it vanish to nothing till my tongue is strawberry-red and stinging.

There's such a jangle of noise in here it's hard to distinguish the melee of music from the screams of the riders. The wind from the sea flaps at skirts and the canopies of ticket booths and the pleated cuffs of the sailors' bell-bottoms. My sister put curling pins in her hair this afternoon and now she holds both hands over her ears to protect her waves, as we negotiate the crowds and stick close to our uncle. I say the names of the rides to myself over and over as I pass them. To remember. And to tell my sad little brother in Canberra who couldn't come. I wonder, looking around me at the unashamed hedonism of the riders, what my mother would think about a place entirely devoted to the pursuit of pleasure and devoid of any educational merit. In a bucket on the tip of an octopus' tentacle, I'm lifted into the darkness of the sky, leaving my stomach behind. I soar high enough that I can look down and see the glitter of the park. The Big Dipper's lights snake and undulate over the scaffolding below. Then just as suddenly I'm swept downward to dip almost to the sea. I fear my shoes will brush the dark rippling surface. But before there's time to worry, I'm high among the stars again, not really daring to look up or down this time and half-hoping the ride will stop. When it does, I alight quickly from the still-swinging carriage. I feel sick and breathless as I look in panic for my uncle. I shouldn't have finished my icecream – I can feel its coldness sitting near the entrance to my stomach. If I don't stop thinking of it, I'm going to be sick. I swallow hard and breathe deeply.

My sister and I thought we'd be allowed two rides, or three at the most. We're astonished at our uncle's extravagance and generosity as he buys reel after reel of lolly-pink tickets. We pass the Merry-Go-Round. To cover the engines inside, there are vertical panels of paintings showing maidens in flowing dresses that brush the grass in the meadows they run through; and rural scenes behind them. Circlets of roses adorn the hair of some who lean against the trunks of trees or recline amid flower-strewn grasses. My sister and I stand and stare. On one of the scenes there's a notice that reads 'Wright and Harts New Steam and Electric Riding Gallery'. Our uncle and his daughter, who've passed by hand-in-hand toward the Ghost Train, turn and look. Our uncle raises his eyebrows and walks back. Half-embarrassed we step onto the platform. We ride alongside small children on our spotted horses and hold the cold smeared brass of the barley-sugar poles. Later we glide through the dank silent interior of the River Caves, shrinking back as skeletons spring forward and dioramas of Eskimos and jungles are revealed at the turn of every corner. A jumble of sounds bursts forth when we finally emerge. Nearby, teenagers are tumbling about, screaming, in a large wooden barrel. One tall youth manages to stay upright by holding his hands flat above him and rotates, star-shaped, for several minutes as we watch. He looks hard at my sister and she turns suddenly and walks ahead of me. Sailors clatter up steep stairs with their girls, to come hurtling down curving wooden slippery-dips on tattered hessian bags. And in the background there's the wailing crescendo of adventurers on the Scenic Railway. We look in mirrors that reflect us as grotesque dwarfs with hips as wide as chests of drawers and skittle legs. In one of them, I see myself looking strangely like my mother – tall and pencil-thin with a long adult face.

Our uncle takes us to the Penny Parlour. I put a coin in a machine and stand on tiptoe. With the wind off the harbour fluttering the skirt round my legs, I turn a handle and watch flickering yellow photographs that riffle like dog-eared pages of an old book. I see lecherous-eyed masters chase simpering servant girls in pantaloons and whale-boned corsets, through Edwardian parlours. Our uncle doesn't come on all the amusements. Just the River Caves. We rush back to him after each ride. He stands in his tweed jacket holding his pipe and watching the teenagers scuffling and daring each other to further excesses and the sailors with their girls. And the girls watch him. With lingering backward glances. Finally we leave and walk down to the ferry. I look back for a last glimpse to where the sea wind tunnels now through the thin crowd inside. My sister turns too and points:

'Oh, look! How *rude* – read Luna Park backwards!'

On our first Sunday morning, before the other two are awake, I dress and leave the house. I want to take the steep path that winds through the front garden and see for myself the tiny landing where the ferry pulls up for its courtesy stop. Once off the stairs from the verandah, I step onto a pathway that weaves through loquats and agapanthus with such sudden turns that, at no time, can you see more than a few feet of track in front of you. Tall straight red-gums predominate, thickly clustered. Their leaves are vermilion and their trunks a delicate pink. I touch the rough morning-cool bark on some, and break into a half-run with the pull of the sloping land. I can smell the pungent sweetness of ginger lilies and frangipani. I listen as I pass, to the drowsy harmony of bees that hover around some swathes of lavender in a small clearing. I think I can hear a ferry approach. So I continue my downward trek, braking once, my arm around the timeless girth of a Moreton Bay fig. I peep through the spiky leaves of some palms that grow at the bottom of the garden, just as the small ferry, with its rippling wake, glides, engines off, to thud gently against the landing and to come to a halt. A woman steps high from the almost silent craft, with the assistance of her companion. They walk along the leafy laneway by the water's edge. Their voices, quite loud and bright at first, in the silent freshness of the morning, diminish as their figures recede and finally disappear from my sight. The water near the bank is dark with a canopy of overhanging foliage. Some pollen that's fallen creates a brocade surface of pale green. Some of the leaves are low enough to brush the rail of the landing. When you watch closely there's still a slight rhythmic lapping-movement around the piers, from the passing ferry. I look across to the grey-green hinterlands of another cove. This is how Captain Cook must have felt. Or more likely an Aborigine who peeped between ancient trunks, saw the taut rippling of those multi-sailed masts in the distance, and thought she must still be dreaming.

The birds you hear most frequently down this way, are doves. But now and then there's the sudden melancholy call of a currawong. I look at my watch. It's only eight o'clock. I have a chance to lie down and think in this hiatus time. Something I've missed a little since Acton with its plentiful places for retreat and reflection. I rest on the jumper I brought and look up at a lacy network of leaves far above. In the gaps there's sky with intermittent fragments of cloud. Like slow-sailing strands of angora. Lying here, in the cat-lazy warmth of the mottling sun, I'm becoming aware of sounds nearby. A woman's voice from next door whose syllables are separated by the blue morning and whose phrases peak and dip as she moves, calls to someone:

'You toss . . . tie my shoe-lace . . . hey, it's warm already . . . well, whose serve?'

I watch an ant crawl up the stalk of a flannel daisy near my head then change its mind and come down again. Then the 'putt' and 'whoosh' of the game begins next door. And the faint scud of swift feet on en-tout-cas. The children on the other side are up and playing in their garden. A small voice is suddenly raised in outrage:

'That's not *fair* – I got it first – I'm telling on you!'

I can smell my aunt's coffee, even from here. I'm so still and quiet as I enjoy my solitude, that twice, a bird steps close and scratches in the leaves only feet away. Others sit high and call to each other in the confines of the garden. So strange in contrast to the magpies who carol across the wastelands of the Acton flats. I leave, and avoiding the narrow path on my right, push my way through low branches, brushing the blue agapanthus with my bare shoulders. I remember my jumper and run back. A community of ants has taken up residence on the side that touched the ground. I shake it and beat it against a tree trunk. Leaves cascade on my hair and a group of birds above, takes off with an explosion of wings. I feel an unaccustomed elation – almost a release – as I cut across the shade-stippled apron of grass directly below the verandah. I pause at the small fishpond to see if its occupants will surface just for me. Then I touch for good luck, the pewter jardinière that brims with pale gold solandra, and continue up the side path by the house. Alamander plants, staked and tied back, spread flat along the sun-white, hot stone wall. As I pass the kitchen window, legs still aching from my ascent through the garden below, I see my aunt's perfectly proportioned figure. She has her back turned to the window and I watch for a moment. I can see a bowl of black olives near her elbow and just then I remember the visitors that are coming this afternoon.

We watch our aunt's guests as they sip from tall frosted glasses and choose tiny delicacies from wooden platters around them. Some stand in the recesses of the dining room while others sit in the half light and shade near the door where the room meets the verandah. A tall woman with hoop earrings, bends low to offer me something from a heaped Florentine bowl:

'A soupçon of avocado, my dear?'

I release my intertwined hands from round my legs and look

up at her: 'Thank you – I love it.'

I don't know what she's talking about. I take a piece of something from a toothpick and start eating immediately to cover my ignorance. She disappears along the verandah between the relaxed artistic figures that recline in deck chairs and lean on the railings far above the fish pond. I look at the morsel of avocado, and take another small bite. It doesn't really taste of anything at all. The pale cream of the flesh has a curve in it of such perfect geometry that I imagine there must have been a stone there once. Then the yellow turns so delicately to palest grass-green, there's no delineation at all. My sister wiggles closer to me:

'Don't chew with your mouth open and don't *smell* everything between bites . . . you shouldn't *inspect* food, you should *eat* it.'

I wish I could know what it's like to be hungry like her. And how to conduct myself socially. My sister talks politely to those who take the trouble to join us briefly and to ask us about Canberra. She even jumps up occasionally and steps through into the hubbub in the dining room to say a few words to someone and to offer food, then to return. I watch a woman younger, I think, than my aunt. She's sitting on a brilliant candy-pink cushion on the verandah a few feet away. If I must grow up I want to be exactly like her. She wears a sleeveless black linen dress and little copper button earrings. Her hair is the colour of butterscotch and she's thin with brown arms. She holds a small triangular glass with an olive in the bottom. Now and then the wind from the garden lifts the hair from the nape of her neck, showing vulnerable white skin where her tan fades. She gesticulates to make a point, and leans forward slightly as if to lend weight to her statement. She's very sure of what she's saying. I never will be. And I'll never have long brown fingers with rings on three of them. My sister is looking at me again:

'And don't *stare*.'

At five o'clock I pluck up enough courage to go through the

dining room to the kitchen beyond. A friend of my aunt's is sitting on the edge of the table. She swings a leg and talks while my aunt rinses glasses. I take a cloth and listen while I dry. Her friend is tall and gracefully angular. She wears black leotards and what looks like two bright paisley tea-towels pinned at the shoulders. One back and one front. She's not old but she has silvery hair that's bunched roughly into a sort of chignon. But wisps of it fall down to frame her face with its triangular green eyes. She wears dull pewter chains round her neck that drop into the folds of the tea-towels. Her large hands are mobile as she talks and her pale green nail polish glows against the colour of her skin. All her movements are quick and full of vitality. I'm glad I'm here. It's good to have something to do. It's lovely that people will start going home soon. My aunt's friend pushes a strand of silver hair behind her ear:

'Well, you've done it again, old girl – that salmon was absolutely superb.'

She makes an 'O' with her finger and thumb, kisses it and continues breathlessly, her voice rising higher over the sound of the water that's hissing into the sink. I can't take my eyes off her. She leans a little so my aunt can hear:

'Did you see old what's-his name with the corporation out in front – you know – Monica's latest friend? You'd think he'd never seen food before in his life. I think she must starve him.'

She breaks off to giggle:

'Of food, I mean, what did you think I meant.'

My aunt, who's been wordless till now, says serenely, still rinsing:

'I didn't think you meant anything.'

Her friend shrieks so loudly I nearly drop a glass:

'You're so *droll* – and the best cook in Sydney. Well my pets, as they say in the classics – I must piss off. See you tomorrow – a little the worse for wear, I fear . . .'

And she's gone, her tea-towel top a bobbing splash of colour in the half-light of the back garden. My uncle is in the doorway now with more glasses and my sister follows him with another tray. My aunt turns from the sink and takes a fresh towel to wipe her hands:

'Well, I can assure you I won't be cooking tonight. You lot can concoct something avant-garde from the left-overs. I shall play with a poached egg at a much later hour.'

I return to my retreat on the floor of the verandah and look through the wire mesh beneath the rail. The garden, which this morning held only sunlight and stillness, echoes with talk and laughter from a group who have spilled outside to seek the shelter of its cloistering trunks and umbrella of leaves. A little apart from the others, a couple sit very close together. I can just see through the trees, that he has one arm around his companion's waist. He kisses her on her mouth and she looks across at the group nearby before responding with a caress to his cheek. I feel a prickle of discomfort and anxiety. I watch them stand up and walk down to the right, through the trees toward the water. Suddenly I think of Ian Holden and the matchbox and I thrust the idea away as quickly as it came. But it intrudes again, unbidden. Then I take solace in the thought that nothing like that could happen in the innocence and serenity of this garden. But Ian Holden said that people don't only do it in bed. But I don't necessarily believe him . . .

'Hey, come back – where were you?'

My uncle stands next to me. I follow the velvet of his trousers then up to his face which peers down at me. He's leaning both elbows on the railing in front of him, hands clasped. Then he looks quickly back into the garden, to the right, and I know that we just shared something – that he was watching them too.

It's half past nine in the morning. We have about forty-eight hours left in Sydney. My sister dresses in the quiet bedroom. The blinds are still drawn and the room greyish and mellow. She turns her back to remove her pyjama top. Then she reaches under her pillow to take out the rumpled little brassière she hides there at night. She knows that I know about it. But concealing it has become a habit. Our mother doesn't wear one and might sneer or laugh if my sister left it around in the open. I feel sad for my sister at home. She even has to wash it secretly and hang it through the window at night to dry. I'm glad I'm not the oldest. Back still toward me, she puts on the brassière. Then slips her dress over her head and turns, pulling down her pyjama pants and stepping out of each leg in turn. She replaces them with her second last pair of clean undies from her case. I know why she waits till her dress is on to clothe her bottom half. It's so that I won't ever glimpse the hair. I have some starting too but I snip it off as it appears. I'm not sure, but I think cutting it could discourage the growth and finally it will just give up and stop.

My sister suggests a walk, so we breakfast and wash up. My cousin is at school, our uncle at his office and my aunt has taken the ferry to town with some drawings. The house is strangely silent. I have a better opportunity to appreciate its now-familiar, characteristic smells when it's empty. There's that pervasive citrus scent in here with the window open and the curtain floating in and out. And the still-fresh coffee smell from grounds in the sieve. I put my head out for a moment to feel the warmth from the slight wind that always blows along this way – funnelled by the side wall of the house and fence. Below the window, purple iris petals flap like spaniel's ears. I leave the kitchen and pass the bathroom. There's the fragrance of recent showers and my uncle's shaving soap. In the passage the seagrass smell gradually predominates as you move toward the dining room. The paper balls above the table hang motionless, their reflections pale half-moons on the dark glossy surface beneath. I cross to sink into one of the leather chairs. I want to preserve the memory of this room. I lean back and stare around me. The shutters of my eyelids click and it's captured. All I can see now, leaning back, eyes shut, is the images of the room. Squares, rectangles and circles of greyish white against the membrane no-colour that covers my eyes. Suddenly the phone peals twice. Shatteringly. And I listen as my sister talks to my aunt in the hallway:

'No, it's me . . . yes we did . . . no, we tried your friend's cumquat marmalade . . . oh, thanks awfully . . . *I think* I know . . .

the lemonade's in the fridge and the chocolate biscuits are in the cupboard to the right?... oh, the left... thanks... well, we thought we'd go for a walk... yes, alright... around three o'clock.'

I join my sister in the hall and she grabs my arm and laughs:
'She said we mustn't forget our elevenses – as if we could! Chocolate biscuits and lemonade!'

Then her face falls and she says quietly:
'Our second *last* elevenses.'

My sister and I walk down the front garden. We discover a small path that leads steeply upward, alongside the ferry landing and past our aunt's frontage. After five minutes, we find ourselves at the top of a rise. Up here there are hydrangeas – out of place somehow, because they're not in someone's garden but seem to be growing wild. We must be on top of a cliff, but any view there may be is obscured by bushes. With a sense of something impending, we sit on a cold stone bench at the side of the path. The knowledge that our visit's nearly over hangs, almost palpably, between us. I think I mind less than my sister, about returning to Acton. I have in my case a box of charcoal sticks and some heavy new drawing paper bought for me by my aunt. And in the same bag an exciting new pen called a Ball-point. Mine's green ink and you never have to fill it – a little ball bearing on the tip spreads the colour as you write or draw. Yesterday, my aunt bought me a book of sketches too, by an artist called William Dobell. I stood in the art shop and it was hard to believe my eyes as I turned each page. You couldn't see the outlines of the people he'd drawn – just their shapes done in a sort of rough scribble. The effect was stunning. My aunt took the book from my hands. Instead of replacing it on the shelf, she actually had it wrapped up and casually handed it to me as we left the shop. She didn't pay money, but the man in charge wrote something in a book and talked a lot to her while we were busy looking around. Everything I see now, I imagine drawing with a rough scribbled outline.

As we sit up here sheltered from the wind, pigeons alight beside us. The soft throb of their voices seems synonymous with the mood of the morning. Some of them are dark grey with greenly iridescent collars – almost peacock coloured – and shimmering as they move their heads. Others are bright russet with white rings around their eyes. Like the reinforcements we use on our foolscap paper at the high school. I'm going to save drawing these birds till Acton. I can see the finished product pinned to the dining room wall. We should have brought some bread. One pigeon is pure seagull-white but without a gull's pale penetrating stare. I suppose birds that have to look into the depths of the sea for their food develop ruthless-looking eyes, while the doves here that depend partly on the benevolence of passers by, can afford to have gentler expressions. As the seat beneath our skirts grows less cold, my sister and I talk about Acton and how far away, how long ago it seems. We list our experiences in Sydney in order of preference. It's almost impossible to decide. My sister loved riding on the bonnet of the jeep. I liked the visit to Pinchgut Island where we stepped down into tiny bleak dungeons lived in by convicts. And Wentworth House – a place of breathless Victorian calm and chilling secret staircases; of echoing tapestry-hung dining halls and white marble-eyed statues. And of course the house itself – in Kareela Road – must come near the top of the list. We agree that the final judgement will come after our trip to town tomorrow.

My sister and I leave the seat then and the pigeons flap off in all directions. Further along the path, we turn a corner and the tall bushes thin out. Together we catch our breath. Sydney Harbour opens below us. The wind pastes our skirts against our thighs as we stand and look. Wide cerulean waters, like a stretch of finely shirred silk, are flecked with the miniature white sails of yachts and indented by the crescents and parabolas of the harbour's many bays. Then further out still, we distinguish dark serrations on either side where, almost at the horizon, the waters meet the open sea – the ocean – the most prolific sculptor of all.

We spend our last day walking the hard pavements of Pitt and Castlereagh Streets. Our aunt buys us coffee and waffles with caramel sauce at Cahill's. Then we set off for David Jones to buy the material our mother instructed us to choose for our new dresses. Our aunt leaves us while she goes off to browse in China and Glass. We find that it's impossible to select anything without our mother in mind. We touch fabric with soft printed pastel bouquets of flowers and garlands of roses that wind through green cotton trellises. But finally we select what we feel our mother would most approve. My sister buys three yards of pale blue cotton twill with navy sprigs of flowers. I'm so confused, I take identical material – but in a different colour scheme – mustard yellow with tiny brown bunches. Our mother's favourite colours are blue and yellow. She says she likes them because they're the colours of the sun and sky. My sister reminds me that we must buy a present each for those at home.

On our final morning by the harbour, I wake at five. I watch a vertical slit of dawn sky beside the blind, brighten to a yellow rod as the sun comes up. I look across at my sister. She's awake too. She always lies on her left side. I asked her why once and she told me that she's more comfortable on her right, but if she lies on the side she least prefers, she can afford to indulge herself in more important ways through the daytimes. Sacrifice, self-denial and limits, she explains, are essential in her philosophy. I'm sad that she has to feel that way.

At Central Station, after our farewells to every room at Kareela Road, we stand in a knot together beside the door to our carriage. Wrapped in my coat that I carry under my arm, is my cousin's doll. The one with the long brown hair that sat on a tiny chair by the bed. My cousin gave it to me with no regrets, even handed it to me by one of its perfectly formed plaster legs while the doll's pretty hair brushed the carpet. My urgent desire for the beautiful little doll was stronger – just – than my embarrassment at being thirteen, and still loving dolls. My uncle has his arms round my sister and me and for once our cousin doesn't look jealously at him.

We step up and turn to stand in the doorway looking down. My aunt starts slightly as the engine gives its warning whistle. Then she turns back to my sister:

'Tell your mother I'll write first. And give your poor father our love and we all hope he's feeling better these days.'

Later, as the train sways homeward and we try to pinpoint landmarks we noticed on the way, my sister turns from the window:

'I wonder what she meant – I hope your poor father's better.'

She looks at her watch:

'Oh well, we'll know in two hundred and forty-eight minutes and ... fifteen seconds.'

The hours pass. We look out at clumps of eucalypts that give way then to undulating hills. The isolated homesteads with their wind-pumps are less frequent now. We open our packages of food from Kareela Road. My aunt has given us sandwiches of brandied pâté. And stuffed eggs and anchovies. My sister's eyes are wet as she takes a first nibble of her rainbow all-day-sucker. Our uncle would have put those in.

At Goulburn, the country flattens out a little. As we near home, I notice the patterns of light have changed and are longer across the sweep of yellow hills.

Finally, our train draws slowly into Canberra's rural station. My eyes scan the sprinkling of figures who stand waiting. A small boy in a red sweater jumps up and down and scuffles near the edge of the platform. His father dashes forward and grasps the child's jumper from the back, till it's stretched into a point. I see my little brother first – my quiet, sometime friend with whom I still make cubby houses and play cops and robbers. Then my parents who stand together but slightly apart from each other. Seeing them with sudden objectivity, I notice how different they look from the families nearby. And there's my big *brother*! Home from the farm, curly brown hair stirred by the motion of the passing train. They're half obscured for a moment, by a wraith of steam from the engine up ahead. We climb out and run back toward them. I put my case down. My throat is aching with the tears I'm trying so hard to hold back. Astonishing, unexpected tears. I put my arms round my mother's waist, my head on her flat chest. I'm unable to utter one word. I can see, next to my eye, the bruise of a shadow in the crook of her elbow. Her dark hair, so like my aunt's, brushes my cheek. She speaks softly for once, a puzzled smile in her voice:

'You strange child! Didn't you *like* your holiday?'

16
FANFARE FOR POTLIDS

We find that in our absence, our father has applied for a transfer to the University of Melbourne. Melbourne! The city of gardens or is it churches? A place I can only imagine from learning about it at school – grey spires on horizons of skyscrapers and a river called the Yarra. Will it be like Sydney but minus the harbour? While our parents talk we collect adjectives starting with 'M' to describe this city that, for our mother, would be more appropriately spelled MECCA. My sister looks out of the window at Canberra's slowly descending dusk:

'Magical, magnificent Melbourne – a momentous event.'

And I wonder what she's really thinking. My little brother silently brings the dictionary:

'Metempiric Melbourne,' he says haltingly, then gives its definition:

'Philosophy of things outside the sphere of experience; believer in this.'

At dinner we talk about the change and what it will mean. Our mother's joy and triumph are transmitted to us all that evening. She sits at the end of the table, fork in hand but her stew almost untouched:

'Well children, you'll find huge department stores, bookshops and libraries everywhere . . . trams and trains . . . and I'm sure you'll make friends in such a big place – it'll be like Brisbane but not oppressively hot – but I don't suppose you remember Brisbane too well.'

She stares thoughtfully through the little dining room window, fork still poised. I look too. There's the bungalow and the familiar rise of grass beyond; and still further the dense clusters of leaves that stir as they hang from gigantic gum-trees beside

124

Acton Road. But what about our father? I mop up Irish stew with a crust of white bread. Won't he miss the Film Society he started and his colleagues from the University? And the beautiful bike rides to the mountains and hills? And his favourite view and the garden he had rotary-hoed and then planted with fine English lawn?

My mother whistles as she washes up and finally, unable to contain herself, breaks into song:

> *'Coming in on a wing and a prayer,*
> *Coming in on a wing and a prayer,*
> *Though with one motor gone, we will still carry on,*
> *Coming in on a wing and a prayer.'*

She stops washing for a moment:

'We may even be able to get a university house this time, with a phone, and an indoor lavatory and a few mod cons.'

My father takes a striped tea-towel from the rail on the back of the door and crosses to the sink.

'I haven't got the job yet.'

He dries the dishes – pushing the towel into the farthest recesses of each glass then twisting so the cloth makes maximum contact. He holds the tumbler to the fading light to look for smudges. Slowly and reflectively. I sit drawing scribbly outlines of birds and people and try to absorb the shock of the changing world around me. After the first excitement, I'm having misgivings.

That night, while I wrestle with my homework, I remember a conversation my parents had weeks ago, before they'd organised the Sydney trip. At the time I'd felt cold fear as my father spoke. They'd been sitting together late at night and hadn't known that I couldn't sleep. I lay in my bed, across the passage and listened. First I heard my father sigh, then he spoke very sadly but with a sort of agitation. I could imagine him, in his worn wing-back chair – perhaps turning his book over on his lap to keep his place:

'Sometimes I wake feeling grey and alien . . . it's as though the fine detailed weave of life has coarsened and expanded . . . and I've fallen – almost – through its mesh.'

I heard him pause to strike a match then he continued in a strange voice:

'Or the weave becomes so coarse I'm in a *void* and can't even see the boundaries of the square of one component of the weave . . . sorry to burden you . . . I know you try to understand and you're patient, God knows.'

All my mother had said, after a long silence, was:

'Oh *Norman*, oh dear me.'

I've heard the expression 'a change is as good as a holiday.' My mother might well feel that moving to Melbourne will benefit my father; will stop him thinking he's going to fall through the hole in the material and never be able to climb back up again. My mother has made the best of Canberra, but she never stops talking about the icy cold winters and the abysmal lack of culture. She makes a sort of joke about it and uses exaggerations and humour to cover her true feelings. But we all know how real, how almost torturous it has been for her during the past three and a half years. But there again, perhaps my father chose to change his life *himself*. Because they never discuss these things with us, I don't know.

Our big brother has come home from the farm. He plays cricket with us on the Acton flats at weekends. He helps my father prune the fruit trees. He plays hide and seek with my brother and me. But we can always find him easily. He's so big there are always bits of his legs or arms sticking out from wherever he's crouching. He has a new job. He's a messenger boy for the Attorney General's department and works in Westblock, adjacent to Parliament House. Mostly he goes to External Affairs and departments nearby. But sometimes he pedals down Canberra's roads and across paddocks with his important information. He dislikes the idea of Melbourne and says he might work on another farm somewhere near Canberra. In the absence of traditional deities and heroes, he's our god. He is seventeen.

Eight weeks after our return from Sydney when I've almost pushed the thought of a future in Melbourne out of my mind, my father, home from college, rides his bike down our drive. It's four o'clock in the afternoon. He travels so quickly that when he brakes at the step to the fly-door, his back wheel slews across the gravel, scattering an arc of tiny stones and dust.

My little brother and I are sitting in the elaborate two-storeyed cubby of pine logs and hessian we made last weekend. It's just light enough that we can see each other's faces. Through one of the slits in the wood, we've observed in the brilliant light outside, our father's unusually rapid descent from road to house, and we smile at his uncharacteristic behaviour. I can see through another gap my sister and her friend swinging in the hammock on the verandah down at the front of the house. No doubt the Ferret is having more adventures. You can't actually see all of the hammock – just the knot around the railing. When it moves a little, you know they're either giggling so hysterically they could fall out at any moment, or perhaps one of them has a foot on the boards and jogs herself as she speaks.

I can even hear parts of my parents' conversation from the kitchen. My mother's speaking louder than usual. I have some paper and a new pen I got last week, which has bright green fluid in its glass handle and a bubble which moves up and down, depending on the angle you hold the pen. When you pick it up to dip the nib in ink and to draw, the bubble slowly ascends to the end, sometimes dividing into two smaller ones. Today we're drawing graveyards. In the grey light, my brother's sheet of paper reflects up onto his face. He has his right arm arched over the top of his drawing so I can't copy any of his gruesome inspirations. The grocer's box we rest our paper on, wobbles a bit as we fill in the details of headstones, straggling grass and railings trimmed with fleur-de-lis. I'm about to draw a ghost, rising turnip-shaped from one of the slabs ranked across my page, when I look up alarmed at a sudden noise. I see through the bright slit, my mother running outside from the dining room. She bangs together two of her pot-bellied saucepan lids. Her behaviour is so strange, I feel a familiar stab of terror in my stomach. Something I haven't felt as badly since Auchenflower when she would appear suddenly, with the copper-stick. She stands looking around. Observes movement from the hammock. And detects a sound from our cubby, because she looks our way. Then half-laughing, half-shouting she resumes her banging:

'Who wants to leave Snake Gully?'

17
THE CHANGES

We arrived in Melbourne last night. It was seven o'clock on January the twentieth, 1949. Two days before my little brother's eleventh birthday. My father starts work at Melbourne University in March and in the meantime we have to find somewhere to live. We have no chance of renting a university place but there's the possibility of a house in a suburb called Caulfield.

I'm lying in a narrow bed in the Victoria Palace in the centre of town. I can hear the unfamiliar sounds of early traffic all around. I look across at my sleeping sister and brother. There's a tall narrow window a few yards beyond the foot of my bed. It sheds through its curtains, a rectangle of greyish light. I turn back the covers and step onto cold linoleum. When I part the flowered drapery, I see outside a sky of silvery charcoal, and my heart sinks. In Canberra the sky was almost always bright blue. We're on the fourth floor. There are high grey buildings all around me and between two of them I can read: 'art to be thrif' on a wall in the distance. It must be part of a slogan. I let the curtains drop back into place and crawl into my bed. I lie there waiting for the others to wake.

I remember our last days in Acton, and the sadness of leaving the shell of the house at 14 Acton Road. We trod the floor of the echoing dining room, bereft of its furniture. Then the passage to the sitting room and bedrooms with their cold dead fireplaces and the square of naked clean boards where our blue carpet had lain. And the dark tableless kitchen – suddenly bigger – with its pantry of blank shelves. While our mother outside – and wearing a hat – touched her favourite plants and, through habit, pulled a weed here and there, I remember my father untied the hammock and folded it as mathematically and meticulously as you *can* fold a hammock. I think it was only at that moment that I realised our move from Canberra was irrevocable. And I looked down at the Acton flats then and back to our sloping garden – the scene for so long of games of 'Fly' and 'Pick a Colour' and 'I am a Soldier Brave'; and of picnics in our musty, humid tent, on its square of yellow grass down near the old pine tree. And the cats! I can't bear to think about the cats. We rubbed our faces on their terra cotta noses. My sister even kissed one of them on its lips and put some liver on her wrist so when it licked and bit her hungrily, she'd sustain the scar from her wound for a lifetime. We brushed and caressed them till their fur was sleek and clung to their bones. They looked half their usual size. And we stroked them hard till they struggled low-to-the-ground to get away. One even hissed at us in protest.

It's funny how things seem more precious when you've lost them.

When the others wake, we explore the streets of Melbourne. I'm determined to find the rest of that slogan I noticed from the window. Finally, I see it, written in aqua cursive script under the name of the store: 'Mantons – it's smart to be thrifty.' The excitement of flickering neon, of cafés and toy shops and dress boutiques, soon dispels much of our homesickness. We enter the Regent picture theatre's rococo foyer to find unparalleled vulgarity and splendour in its carpeted horse-shoe staircase – its maroon velvet, and gilt plaster statues. And next door but downstairs, the Plaza cinema, almost as richly ornamented. In Myers, my sister discovers that you can run up things called escalators – face to face with people travelling down. My little brother and I watch her from the bottom. Then he tries to copy her but collides with a woman carrying parcels. She drops them and they fall onto one of the slotted steps and are carried down to accumulate on the last stair. People alighting falter and trip in an attempt to circumnavigate the packages. A man in uniform walks quickly across to pacify the customers who are shouting at my sister and brother. My sister looks up at the officer with a facsimile of despair on her face:

'Please, my brozzer and I . . . ve com yesterday from Poland . . . ve cannot read ze English so good . . . ve leeve in a tiny veellage vhere zay haf not got ze . . . travelling steps . . . all ve *looking* for iss some food . . . ve are so *very* hungry.'

We escape into the street and make a dash for a shop called Buckley and Nunns next door where we collapse with laughter into bolts of material on a stand.

In Collins Street my sister dares me to approach someone with a phrase she read on a poster in the grounds of a church in Canberra. One she's never forgotten. I feel weak-kneed with fright and I can taste the fear in my mouth – but her bribe of ninepence gives me courage. A man sits at the top of the steps of the General Post Office. Its the longest walk I've ever taken. Half-way up I've forgotten how the sentence goes and I have to go all the way down to ask my sister. Up at the top now I tap the man's black serge shoulder and whisper, dry-mouthed:

'Have you accepted Christ Jesu as your saviour?'

He looks at me, uncomprehending. I have to retreat but I can't run down again in case he decides to chase me, so I find myself in a long cool corridor with archways on my left and post boxes on my right. My sister and brother walk sedately, innocently, up the stairs toward me, my sister detouring slightly to brush the man's shoulder with her hand. Lightly, as if by accident. When we reach the end of the corridor of pillars we look back. The man stares after us. A hundred yards further down Elizabeth Street we turn to see that he's still staring.

We return to the Victoria Palace. Our mother is waiting in the lounge and looks up from her reading when we rush through the glass doors:

'I hope you've enjoyed yourselves, children – I'll hear about it over lunch – by the way, it's on the university so choose what you'd really like.'

She tells us that our father is looking through the house in Naroona Road, Caulfield, and will be going to Parkville in the afternoon to meet his new academic colleagues.

'I suppose it's nice enough in its own way.'

My mother stands in Naroona Road on the footpath outside number thirteen. Her hand is on the wire gate which she's about to push open. We see before us a tiny garden measuring about forty feet across the front, and a small timber house set not twenty feet back. There aren't the crests and mounds of grass – the sloping, treed lawns and dwarfing gums we're used to at home in Acton, so we keep our counsel. Our mother looks down at our faces:

'It's only until we find something better – it won't be forever – we must live *somewhere*, children.'

We approach the small wooden porch up a dead-straight concrete path from the gate. A prickly pear, growing alongside, towers over us. My mother looks to right and left as she walks slowly. I think she's seeing it with her circular beds of jonquils, her grape hyacinths and the sheltered spot she'll create for her garden screen.

Inside, there's a small sitting room looking out on the ankle-high grass of the overgrown front garden. Each of the three little bedrooms is Kalsomined in a different pastel shade:

'This primrose one will be for you girls.'

I stand beside my mother and see a yellow room. I thought it would be pale pink. The dining room is quite big and has dark wooden panelling up to the height of my shoulder. My mother pokes her head in and points:

'The piano can go against that wall.'

I run my hand over the shiny boards beside me and see the reflection of my face as a ghostly smear and my dress a pearly smudge. Soon my sister will be playing the 'Moonlight Sonata' in here and I suppose my father will be carving mutton and everything will seem normal again. I can see through the small window, the cream stucco of the house next door only a few feet away over a leaning fence burdened with old ivy and its star-shaped leaves. I find my mother standing in the middle of the kitchen. She's put her bag on the cold gas stove. When you're in the centre of this room you can reach everything – stove, sink and all the cupboards, without moving your feet. She touches the wooden draining board then stands on tiptoe to lean over the sink and to peer through a dirty window whose view is a built-on fourth bedroom with the back door of the house set in its outside wall. Her hand has left a print on the grimy pane:

'This is more a scullery than a kitchen,' is all she says.

I know she's disppointed – that she hates this room where she'll spend so much time. But she can't say too much because it was she who wanted to leave Canberra. My sister turns on the brass tap over the sink, and brown water sputters and jerks out. We step through to the long narrow lean-to. Then outside. The sun is making a supreme, but unsuccessful, effort to reach through the dense bright-edged clouds. My mother sits on the back step, her feet on a cracked uneven concrete path that runs the width of the house. My sister is beside her, resting too. My mother lights a cigarette and puts her bag down:

'Well, it's not *huge* – really I can see it all from here.'

My little brother stands at the corner of the house looking down the side path. His hands are clasped in front of him, arms straight down:

'Look! I'm Donald Bradman!' He swings a phantom bat. 'You little *beauty*, a *six*!'

At least the garden is alright. It's overgrown – but you can see that thought must have been given by someone years ago to its design. It's interesting what some sorts of light – some kinds of days – can do to a garden. I see as I walk forward, every leaf and dark branch, pronounced and clear. There's no shade or wind to seduce your perceptions – to incline you to romanticise. So, although I view a commonplace little garden, it's one that has an indefinable quality about it. Certainly there's nothing magical about the just-discernible rows of withered pumpkins in long grass; about the leaning shed and the fig tree with an empty birdcage hanging from a branch. But I've felt this mood before – in the evenings at home in Acton – when geraniums glowed with a depth of almost euphoric colour and the world seemed still and set. And time had stopped for a moment as you looked down, unbelieving, at clearly-outlined clusters of frost-green Cats Tongues. And stared into the unmoving depths of a vermilion prunus – as though a thin film had been peeled from your eyes.

Suddenly my little brother calls, ahead of me now:

'Hey! Up here there's *more!*'

He stands behind a picket fence with a gap in its palings. I see beyond, gnarled, low trees with shrivelled fruit among their leaves. My mother passes me, stepping high through the long grass. I can just hear her say as she joins him:

'Oh – how quaintly old fashioned to separate the orchard from the rest of the garden.'

Just before we return inside, we find a small door in the weatherboard wall and behind it, a lavatory. I feel a wrench of unbearable pity for my mother who so much wanted an inside toilet. But she says, cheerful now, because of the garden and its potential:

'We'll ask the owner if we can cut a doorway through to it from the lean-to next to the kitchen.'

We have no houses opposite us at thirteen Naroona Road. Just a high wall, which conceals a huge racecourse that stretches across with its white fences, neat well-kept tracks and high grandstands, to the Caulfield Station.

My sister and I start our Melbourne education at MacRobertson Girls High School. On our first day the headmistress tells us in her office that long ago a man called Sir MacPherson Robertson gave forty-thousand pounds from his chocolate-frog factory to start the school. The corridors here are so long. Everything the teachers say is confusing. We notice that Melbourne people use words strangely. The girls say 'I reckon' when they mean 'I think'. There are no men teachers. Not one. I'm baffled by the timetable. You have to look at an enormous notice-board of subjects and times in the mornings and plan your day accordingly. It's so different from Canberra High. Here the girls in my form seem older than me. They buff their nails with emery boards and giggle about boys they know. And in the lunch hour, they gather in knots or walk arm-in-arm around the playground, talking about clothes. We travel to Flinders Street Station by tram to catch the train back to Caulfield each day. I sit looking at my pink fivepenny ticket. Then I turn it over. On the back, in startling red, it says 'Ask for Stamina Self-Supporting Trousers'. Under that is the Thought for the Month: 'What happens does not really matter – it is how you take it'.

Well, I'm not taking MacRobertson Girls High School too well. Looking again at my ticket I realise, as I have so often before, that it's me that's out of place. I think with dread of the day after day after day that I must spend at the new high school. My sister breaks my mood and almost seems to read my mind:

'I don't know . . . girls without boys around seem so terribly *effeminate* somehow.'

After our third day our mother asks our father to pull the strings necessary to enrol us at University High School in Parkville. But we have our blue and white MacRobertson uniforms. And there's no money for the green checks and fawn trimmings of our new summer school dresses. So our mother unpicks the white collars and cuffs and dyes the uniforms. Now they are checked in the unusual combination of dark and pale green. Then she dips the collars and cuffs in weak tea and when they are the right shade of fawn, sews press-studs (she calls them 'domes') on the necks and sleeves of the frocks. She must dye the collars and cuffs every week when she washes the dresses, as of course the cold tea comes out in the copper. We have to wear the black shoes from MacRobertson too instead of the regulation brown. At school my sister and I feel the quiet ridicule in the sideways glances of the other pupils. And finally we approach the offices of the Interstate Taxation in the T and G building in Collins Street. We put our ages up by one year to fifteen and sixteen. As filing clerks from four o'clock till five-thirty, three evenings a week, we soon have the money for our brown shoes which we buy after work at a shop called Whites in Elizabeth Street.

My sister spends much of her weekends writing to her friend in Canberra. Sometimes the letters consist of ten foolscap pages – mostly, I suspect, adventures of the Ferret. I've started to learn the piano again. Every Sunday afternoon I walk the leafy avenues off Glen Eira Road to my lesson. Miss Richardson gives me *The Children's Bach Book* to start with. I practise for an hour each morning before we begin the long train and tram journey to the high school. Sometimes my father stands in the doorway to watch and listen while I struggle to perfect *Anna Magdalena* and the Bach *Chorales*. I looked up to apologise one morning for all my mistakes and hesitations, and I saw that he was crying.

One day he comes into our bedroom quite early before breakfast. A golf ball rests on his outstretched palm. We lie in bed and look at it. Although he'd been a rower at Oxford in his youth, we've never known him to be interested in sport at all, so we wait for him to speak:

'You see before you, my darlings, economy of shape and perfect symmetry,' he says. 'Note the uniform harmoniousness of the indents – the dimples.' He breaks off then and pointing to me, says, smiling: 'No, not the ones in your cheeks.' Then continues, 'A sphere has no beginning – no end – it just IS.'

The ball lies still, a tiny smudge of shadow around its base. Then his large pink palm and fingers close around it and he says over his shoulder, as he leaves our room:

'The circle is a symbol of completion – of wholeness – but as Carl Jung says "the right way to wholeness is made up of fateful detours and wrong turnings".'

My sister and I look at each other and raise our eyebrows uncomprehendingly.

My sister's pulling her creased little bra from under her pillow when he returns. This time he stands in the doorway:

'Have you ever seen a raindrop falling – that is, its shape?'

My sister hastily pushes the bra back under her pillow:

'Well – I s'pose originally, before it hits the ground, it's roundish like the ball – or a sphere pulled out of shape by its descent?'

My father cups his hands, fingers apart and looks down at them:

'Yes, it takes that beautiful round form because of the minute forces of surface tension, which act like a skin and pull all the little bits – atoms – of water into such a perfect shape.'

Then he comes a little further into our room (propelled by his enthusiasm, I think as I watch him).

'And there's something marvellous at the end of some showers of rain.'

At last I can contribute:

'The rainbow?'

He breaks into my reply, such is his excitement:

'All the bright colours have come because the little spheres break up the light into those parts.'

His voice is so loud that I find myself cringing under the bedclothes. With his brows raised so high, the flesh above his eyes is pulled up to reveal the whole of his blue irises. It's hard to listen when I have to watch so carefully the suddenly unusual contours of his face:

'Would you believe! Circles are everywhere in nature! Even in the smallest specks of dust we call atoms, which are like minutely spinning spheres of electricity!'

He's almost shouting now and his face is lit up – but drops a little as my mother passes and looks in:

'Will you let those children get dressed! They'll never catch their train at this rate.'

I've started painting in oils. My father has made me a lovely wooden easel because he says I show promise. I'm not sure that I agree. I can never quite get the effect I want. I draw red and green apples on draped velvet and the part I love most is putting in the little white highlights at the completion of each canvas. I paint the portraits of imagined children too. Solemn chubby-cheeked toddlers with blue eyes. My mother calls them chocolate-box pictures, but stands behind me as I paint and sometimes suggests colours. I love most, laying the brown paint on the crown of the child's head, then bringing it down and adding ochre and cadmium and finally white for the gradual shading towards my imaginary source of light. Last I add enough darkness to the spaces behind the figure to throw it into relief. It's exciting and amazing what you can do with colour.

At University High School I love the English, French and Art periods. And Biology fascinates me. In English we have a text book called *Feet on the Ground*. It has the sorts of poems in it that I haven't seen before. I know all of Robert Louis Stevensons's off by heart and many of Walter de la Mare's. But there's different poetry as well here. One poem starts this way:

> *A snake came to my water-trough*
> *On a hot, hot day, and I in pyjamas for the heat,*
> *To drink there.*

I try writing less traditional poetry than I have before. I submit one to the school magazine – *Ubique*. It appears in the next issue, to my surprise. And alongside it, an adaptation of one of my sister's old Lamptonese pieces. On the same page is a short story by a prefect called Beverley Hayes and another by a boy I've seen in the library called Don Thomas. He signs himself D M Thomas, which seems very sophisticated to me somehow. I'm going to keep the magazine always.

At University High the days are very long. I haven't made a friend, so I sit on a bench under a row of dark pine trees and eat alone at lunchtime. One day some girls sit alongside me, and I notice that the fillings in their sandwiches are different from mine. That's the main problem, I think – that everything about me is so different.

I feel supremely self-conscious and miserable sitting there apart day after day. I wish my mother would give me ham and pickles on my bread like theirs and cut the sandwiches diagonally instead of into two rectangles. I think I'd be acceptable then. One day I pluck up courage I don't really have and, after rehearsing what I'll say for ten minutes, I turn to the girls nearby:

'Could I join you for lunch today?'

They look at me, astonished that the quiet statue has moved. Giggling a little, they move up the bench toward me. One of them, staring hard, even smiles and offers me a Throatie from a red and white packet.

In Melbourne you can buy Chinese food. My mother, who always likes to stay abreast of the trends, buys long yellow pastry things one day, called Chicken Rolls. And some glossy white Dim Sims with little indented checks in the white pastry coating. You eat all of this with soy sauce from a bottle. She's bought the strange food at the Myer Emporium. We sit down and she says, as she opens her table napkin:

'We should be eating all of this with chopsticks really, you know.'

I taste the savoury rolls and the sweetish minced meat inside. It's so extraordinary and so beautiful. And the sauce is black and salty. I usually have to be encouraged to eat, but not tonight. My sister watches disapprovingly as I ask for another Dim Sim. Suddenly my stomach feels cramped and my head tight. I sit toying with the soft white end of the morsel that's left on my plate. It has a little pinched tuck where the Chinese people must have folded the pastry around the meat. I leave the table then and go to the bathroom. I pull down my pants and see, lying on the bridge between the two leg-holes, a small, brown flat autumn leaf. How on earth could it have *got* in there? I didn't feel it scratch me at dinner. I touch it and find that it's wet – not a leaf at all. It's fluid of some sort. I pull up my pants and join the others at the table. My head feels tight again and the ache in my stomach won't go away. I feel such disorientation that when I speak I have to choose my words very deliberately.

I sit there long after the others have left. My mother looks in as darkness starts to fill the dining room:

'Too tired to listen to the Hit Parade?'

I look down at the scarred, scratched familiar table. I can't leave it. With my head still lowered I say to my mother, who's supposed to look after me because I'm only a child:

'I'd like to draw but I'm too tired from school to get some paper.'

So she brings me three sheets of my father's foolscap. I can hear the others talking in the sitting room and the radio plays music. I sit for an hour and a half in the dining room. My mother flicks on the light for me as she passes to make coffee:

'Don't strain your eyes.'

At a quarter to nine I leave the chair and walk slowly, legs together, down the passage to bed. I haven't cleaned my teeth or washed my face, or said goodnight. The drawing paper on the table in the dining room is blank. I pretend to be asleep when my mother looks in. And again when my sister joins me in our bedroom, quietly undresses and slips into bed. If I lie quite unmoving with my legs pressed together, the combination of lack of gravity and my stillness will probably make it go away. I look at my clock at eleven. Then at two. Moonlight fills the room and touches the ends of our beds and the contours of my sister's sleeping body under the blankets. At five o'clock the walls suddenly suffuse with apricot and I realise the sun will soon be up. So will my mother, who doesn't know. And never will. She opens our door at half past six. I look across at her dark face in the doorway without moving a muscle of my body:

'I can't go today. I've got flu.'

She crosses the room to me and puts a warm dry hand on my forehead:

'You aren't hot, darling. Have you got a sore throat?'

I nod. Not because I have, but because her endearment makes me want to cry. Why didn't she talk to me about it before? Why aren't I a boy? My stomach is so sore. She brings me a Bex powder mashed up in honey. She thinks it's for my throat. I stay there for three days, only getting up to go to the lavatory when she's shopping. I won't wear anything for the mess except my pants which are now so stained, that, on the third day I throw them away and wear a fresh pair with toilet paper lining them.

Oh yes, I do remember in Acton her telling us about the flow of blood. But I never dreamed she meant it would apply to *us*. It was always something that only happened to other people. Not me. On the fourth day, a Saturday, my little brother comes into our room and sits on the edge of my bed to scrutinise my face:

'Aren't you *ever* getting up? I'm going to look at the park you can see from the grandstand in the racecourse.'

The lure is irresistible. And of course, we'll be riding there. That'll keep it from coming out. On my beloved, familiar bike I feel better. I tell my brother I have diarrhoea and we stop at every public toilet so that I can make my inspections and stuff my pants with more paper. I feel a rush of despair each time I look and see that it's still coming. That it's true. But there's still the chance that I have an illness and this is one of its symptoms.

We're back home by one o'clock and my mother stares at me with horror:

'Good *God* child – you're so pale and thin!'

Of course I'm thin! I haven't eaten or drunk anything for nearly four days. I thought food and fluids would make it increase.

If I was self-conscious before, now as I ride my bike through the streets of Caulfield and its neighbouring suburb, Carnegie, I feel like a raw nerve. One of the thread-like, dangly ones in my Biology book. I'm taking a sandwich in my pocket down to St Kilda beach. Everyone seems to be watching me. I can see them staring from under my eyelids and I ride faster and faster to get away. A car nearly collides with me at Brighton Road and I almost don't care. When people stand there following me with their critical, judgemental eyes – do they see me as a little girl or as a teenager?

I sit in a small circular shelter on the beach and watch the waves creaming rhythmically over wet sand. No one knows where I am. I throw pieces of my bread to the gulls. The sea stretches before me, extending forever on each side. I suppose you could wade in and just keep going until it's over your head. They tell me a great uncle of mine in New Zealand did that, twenty years ago . . . just kept walking – in his clothes too – and was never seen again. It's funny that life seems so permanent – so immutable. Yet – like a daisy destined for a vase, click! – it's so *easy* to die. You can be riding a bike and a car crushes the life out of you in a matter of seconds.

There are windows all around me, in this little protective house. And the edges of the sea flush over tiny fragile shells nearby then drag back across the ridged sand. Further out where the ships and rusted tankers seem motionless, the water is lead-coloured, and swells as it prepares to hurl itself toward the beach. I sit on the hot narrow slats of the seat in the shelter, and think back to that first night when I found the wet autumn leaf.

The sun is thundering down on the windows of my small beach-dome and even though it's May I feel burning hot. My face is pulsating and I put up a hand to touch my ember-like cheek. My heart is thudding as though I've been running a race. And I watch waves that suddenly have no sound. I look around at the glass that encloses me in here, and I see it burst and shatter outward and tinkle to the sand below. I find my hands are clenched into fists and I expect to see blood on my knuckles. But there isn't any. And the windows are there too, glinting in the afternoon sun. Quite intact and unbroken. I step outside. There's a piece of honeycomb rock nearby. I pick it up and look back at the shelter. Then I hurl the rock as hard and fast as I can toward a seagull that's standing, red legs reflected in the wash of foamy water around it. The stone misses and I sink onto the sand. I've never in my life wanted to hurt a creature before. I look around me, remembering Sandgate when I was eight or nine – almost half my lifetime ago. I stay on the beach all the afternoon. No one's there to stare at me. And no one at home will miss me. Finally, as the sun burns down into the sea with almost audible sibilance, I take my bike and ride through the suburbs and back to the house.

18
THE SANDS SHIFT

I've made a friend. Her name is Bernadette Shannon. She has three brothers and a sister and lives in the street behind ours. My friend is Catholic and her family has religious pictures on the walls. There's a cross-stitched one of Jesus hanging above the mantelpiece in her parents' bedroom. She told me that if you watch the embroidered face for long enough, its eyes will open for a moment. So I sat alone on the white damask bedspread for one long hour on a Saturday afternoon without moving my eyes from those in the picture. I was starting to feel quite religious. Twice I imagined I saw a preparatory flicker beginning. My eyes were sore and dry from not blinking. My friend's younger brother, Patrick Shannon, came into the bedroom then and when I told him I thought it was a trick – that they'd never open – he said that's because they only do it for believers.

Sometimes I go to Mass with the family – much to the amusement of my mother. I haven't got a hat so just before I enter the cathedral I put a hanky on my head. At my friend's place they have different sorts of food. For lunch we might have Strasburg jaffles with tomato sauce and chocolate-flavoured milk to drink. And for dinner, puce saveloys and home-made fried chips with more tomato sauce. Everyone seems to talk at once at their table and the children all have jobs – like cooking, clearing away and washing up. They say grace before eating and even the youngest child is still and quiet at these times.

Bernadette Shannon is fifteen, two months older than me. She has a well-developed figure and loves what she calls 'teenage clothes'. Sometimes we walk across the racecourse to the Caulfield shops and the boys wolf-whistle at us. But I know they're not looking at me. We went into Myers Bargain Basement one Saturday morning recently and bought matching cotton jumpers. They're bright red and have names printed all over them in white. Bing, Gary, Frankie, Ray. Where the sleeves are set into the body, you can see short bits of the names. I hung mine over the chair next to my bed after I bought it so that it would be the first thing I'd see when I woke the next morning. We have long 'New Look' skirts too – they come to our ankles. My mother says the fashion is a reaction to the war, when material was so scarce.

My father has flu. In fact he's had it for two weeks and just lies in bed all day and night. Sometimes before I get up I can hear my mother reading news items from the *Argus* to him. Occasionally he makes a short reply but mostly he's silent. My mother keeps phoning the university to tell them that he's still not well enough to come in. She's even more irritable than usual because she has so much work to do and no one to share it with her. After school my sister and I read to him to try and cheer him up.

I got the book I was hoping for last Christmas. It's called *The Miracle of the Human Body*. So I read him that. With 700 pages, it's heavy and thick with shiny thin paper and illustrations on most pages. There are diagrams of men standing with their heads sideways and bodies facing the front. Some of them show figures with ropey musculature like the skeins of wool my mother winds around chairs to make into balls. And in others, the skeleton and trees of veins and arteries. At the beginning of the book there are pictures and text that tell you what doctors knew about anatomy as early as the sixteenth century. One of my favourites shows a short man in a leaping pose. Every muscle has a tiny letter or number on it. There's Latin printing above and below the etched figure. Behind, in the far background, trees and old castles are drawn intricately and a river snakes into perspective. I decided this morning to see if I can learn anything about influenza in *The Miracle of the Human Body*. Also I want to see if they show or mention the unconscious part of the mind. There's little in it about the former that I don't already know, and nothing at all about the latter. I look round the door of my father's bedroom. He's lying there just the same with the sheet pulled up under his chin, but he's awake so I go in. His eyes move with me as I approach the bed. I'm wearing my red jumper. I stand there and we look at each other. He moves a little and one hand comes over the top of the sheet to point:

'You look like a pillar box.'

His voice sounds very small and far away and has a hollowness. I turn round to show him the back of my jumper. I'm suddenly aware of its vulgarity. I look down at him over my shoulder:

'They're the fashion. They only had white on red or red on white . . . I came in to ask you why my medical book doesn't refer to the unconscious.'

He stares up at me as if he hasn't heard, and I feel a flicker of discomfort and apprehension. Then he smiles a little with his mouth. But his eyes stay sad:

'Could we talk about it when I'm well?' And he pulls the sheet around his shoulder and turns to the wall.

I look then, before I leave, at the small bedside table he made in his workshop in Acton. On a low square of sunlight that comes from under the almost-drawn blind, a book called *Authority and the Individual* lies closed, and beside it, a brown bottle of tablets and a cup half-filled with water. His glasses rest on the book's cover. I hesitate, wanting to offer to read a chapter to him from the book. But his blunt shoulder deters me, so I leave the room, touching the outline of his foot as I pass the end of the bed.

At University High School sport is compulsory. On Friday afternoons you must choose from gymnasium, basketball, volleyball and rounders. After several weeks I go to the sports mistress and ask her if I could use the library. I can't remember the rules of the games to play well enough, and the other girls are always shouting despairingly at me. She tells me that if I'd prefer, ice-skating would be acceptable as a sport. So each Friday, I hire a pair of size seven white boots from the Glaciarium just down from Flinders Street Station in town, and take to the rink. There are few people there at that time of day. For the first few weeks I have many falls, but after that I manage to stay upright for progressively longer periods. The rink is huge. It echoes with the latest popular songs that come over loud speakers all around:

> *'Gee but it's great,*
> *After bein' out late,*
> *Walkin' ma baby back home.'*

The Glaciarium has a very particular cold smell when you enter. Although the ice is dirty and scuffed with tracks and ridges and the circulation in my ankles is practically reduced to nothing, skating is a highlight of my week.

One Friday, when I've just learned to go out into the middle, someone suddenly grabs my hand. I look up into the brown eyes of a tall youth in a blue school blazer. I'm tempted to pull away but too shocked – and flattered – to do so. We skate in silence for a moment. He asks me my name and school and, as I reply, I notice the words 'De La Salle' on his pocket in golden embroidery. 'Of the room' – what an incredibly strange name for a school. He tells me he's sixteen and will do medicine after he matriculates. That evening we catch the 5.48 train to Caulfield. His name is Andrew Moss and he lives in nearby Malvern. We exchange addresses and phone numbers and that night I receive my first call from a boy. I learn that he's an orphan who lives with his sister and aunt. My friend, in the street behind, seeks my company quite often but now her interest is suddenly doubled. She changes the style of my hair which till now, has hung straight around my face. When I go to Luna Park with my new boyfriend, she lends me her black patent shoes with a small heel.

One Saturday night we go to see George Brent and Joan Blundell in a horror film at the Hoyts theatre up in Glenhuntly Road. During the interval he buys a flat box of chocolates. When the lights go down he offers me one. I take the nearest to me, hoping it's a caramel cream and not a jelly. Then he selects one for himself, but as he's extracting it from its tiny brown pattycase, the box tips, spilling the entire contents onto the carpet at our feet. Neither of us acknowledges the accident. Neither of us even looks at the other. The sweets lie there on the floor – and remain when we leave. Testimony to our maturity, our impeccable manners but – more importantly – our sophistication and savoir faire.

Sherbrooke Forest, high in the Dandenong Ranges, is almost an hour's train ride from Melbourne. One Sunday we walk its narrow bush-lined tracks, while moisture from the night before glistens on every leaf and hangs on the underside of the railings of narrow bridges we cross together. Andrew Moss takes my hand. From that moment I walk stiff-legged and breathless with embarrassment, acutely aware of every nerve in my fingers which lie enclosed in his palm. We reach the tiniest waterfall I've ever seen. It's really just bubbles that slip over brown rocks to trickle away into the dark undergrowth. My friend looks around, then puts one arm over my shoulders, and kisses me on my mouth. I try to remember what film stars do. I close my eyes tightly, hoping he'll stop. But he says, after a moment:

'The human heart beats at an average of seventy-two times per minute.'

Then, hesitantly, he puts his hand through the V-neck of my jumper and onto my chest:

'Let's see if yours is beating.'

Well, if it's not, I'd be stretched out in front of him. Stonecold dead. I wouldn't be standing here pink and breathing hard and wishing I could go home. I break away and run through the forest the way we came. He follows. Walking parallel, but several feet apart, we arrive back at the station and take the train home. I don't see a great deal of Andrew Moss after that.

19
UNEXPECTED GUESTS

For my fifteenth birthday, my mother gives me a game of Monopoly. We play in the evenings in Caulfield. My mother is out nearly every night at meetings, so she can't participate. She's helping establish a local branch of the Communist Party in a house up in Carnegie. My father doesn't join our games either. The flu he developed so many weeks ago, doesn't seem to be getting better. Occasionally he goes into the university – a solemn-faced, thinner figure than before. At nights he's in bed long before us and reads or prepares his notes. Sometimes, when I pass his door, I see him propped on the pillows in his bed, just staring down at the blankets. I can tell he's not reading, as his book is turned over in front of him.

One morning, something wakes me. I see that my sister's eyes are open too. She looks across at me unsmiling. Something is happening outside our closed bedroom door. We sit up. It looks so early, it could be dawn. Pale light silhouettes the carved posts of the porch outside our window. Beyond it, the fence and wire gate are dark and outlined by the soft bright sky on the horizon over the racecourse. There's even a streetlight still on but with no halo around its rim. I hear again the small sound I heard before. And our mother's voice, unnaturally clear – and urgent – in the quiet of the morning.

'I can't wake my husband.'

Then silence. I think my heart will stop. I'm unable to move. I try to lever myself out of bed but my arms are jelly. My sister jumps out and runs to pull the door open to listen. Our mother must have heard her because she comes down the short hall and into our room. There's a rhythmic surging in my ears, so loud that I can hardly hear my mother's faltering voice:

'It's been so hard for him to sleep at night.'

She speaks awkwardly, hesitantly. She's trying to explain something. But she's not succeeding. My mother actually seems afraid. She hasn't even put her dressing gown on and I can see her thin brown breast. She turns and crosses quickly to the window. My sister and I sit waiting for her to speak again. But she doesn't. I want to go in and look at my father, but I can't move. Then my mother leaves our room and I hear her voice from across the passage:

'*Come* on, oh dear . . . *please.*'

My sister hasn't moved all this time. She's looking through our open door into the hallway. I notice the little curling wands against her cheeks and suddenly the fact that she put them there last night makes me feel so sad. The rest of her hair hangs round her neck to the collar of her pale pyjama top. She has one foot on top of the instep of the other. We must never, never quarrel again. I hear an engine noise. Then I see a movement through the window and my sister turns too. Uniformed men are running up our concrete path. I hear my mother go to the front door and open it. Indistinct, overlapping voices grow louder. There are scuffling noises in the room across the passage and I hear a man's voice, breathless but sure:

'There's a pulse.'

I see my father, under a blanket on a stretcher. It bobs as two men carry it across the porch outside our window and down the step to the front garden. Suddenly my mother runs towards them. They hesitate. She puts a brown glass bottle into one of their pockets and they continue down the path and through the gate. A minute later there's the clangour of bells from the ambulance – a sound which diminishes rapidly into the distance, far away from Naroona Road.

It's not a winter's day but I feel cold and my hands won't fasten the buttons on my schooldress. I can hear my mother and sister talking in the sitting room in softened voices so that my little brother won't wake.

I watch the sky through the windows of the classrooms at University High while I wait for the final bell to ring and release me. My sister and I travel home together for once. The next day being Saturday, we visit my father. He lies behind screens, in the ward that he shares with three other men. He seems to be asleep, his pale tranquil face in little contrast to the white pillow. His thick silvery hair has fallen onto his forehead. As we sit staring at him, nurses come regularly to hold his wrist, to lift his eyelids and to look closely at him. They smile at us and I feel a little better.

My father stays in Prince Henry's Hospital for several weeks. They give him electric current treatments and sometimes when we visit he has bruises on his shoulders or face. Once his arm is in a sling. As the time goes by, he seems to regain his interest in us and talks of walking in the grounds of the hospital. But he doesn't always remember the things we say about school. I sit on the edge of his bed one day and tell him of my difficulty with logarithms, and how hard it is for me to understand the basis for their use in maths. When we visit him next, he smiles at me, even prods my arm playfully, and says:

'Are you up to logarithms yet? . . . tell me what they're teaching you at that school of yours.'

My sister and I return from University High one afternoon and he's home. But he has to travel to Prince Henry's every Saturday to have more treatments. And he can't return to the University yet.

My mother works now for three days each week at the Caulfield Convalescent Hospital in Kooyong Road. She scrubs out the patients' lockers and mops the floors. She's called a wardsmaid. On the other two days of the week she makes French Flowers. Sometimes I help her. You have to heat up a tiny iron rod with a ball on the end. You cut pastel-coloured silk into petal shapes with a pattern, while the rod is warming on a bead of gas. Then you push the hot iron ball into the material, creating a

150

curve. And you have quite a realistic petal. When you've got four or five of these, you assemble them with wire, making a stem last of all, which you cover with grass-green fabric to look lifelike. My mother read an advertisement about the French Flowers and every week she receives through the mail, cardboard boxes of materials – and a small payment for the work she's done the previous week. At first she found the flowers very difficult. But now I often sit and watch her in the tiny kitchen, as she prepares the iron tool and deftly crafts her small delicate blooms, packing them with care into the containers. My father helps her by doing all the garden. His doctor has told him that he needs fresh air and no books for some time, to give his mind a rest. My sister and I take it in turns to pick him up from the hospital on Saturdays, as he's often confused and upset after the treatments.

One morning when I'd helped him across St Kilda Road, he started to get undressed – taking off his shoes first and very carefully placing them neatly together under the tram shelter seat. I was able to stop him after he'd removed his coat and jumper. I suppose he thought he'd come across the road the opposite way and had to get into bed. My mother told us that he suffers from a disease called Melancholia. That it may come and go for the rest of his life. He takes white tablets called Largactil. At home he's often quite angry about the French Flowers and is always threatening to write to the man who runs the business. He calls him a slave-driver, a profiteer and an exploiter of humanity.

We have a boarder too. My sister and I have moved into the dining room, that now has a tall bookshelf to bisect it at the window, making two unusual little rooms. And the dining table and chairs are crammed into the sitting room. It's the first time I've ever had a room to myself – well, half a room. It looks out on the ivy-covered fence I saw on the day we first inspected the house. And my sister and I can still call to each other over the top of the shelves. We buy bed lamps from Coles. They have little fluted translucent blue shades. My sister calls her half of the room 'The Boudoir'.

Our paying guest is a theology student aged twenty-two. Our

mother has warned us that while he's in the house or eating with us at dinner, that we must never swear. He's very tall, with dark hair and grey eyes. He's the quietest, most gentle man I've ever met. His name is James Franklin. When he walks to the station in the mornings I hurry to get ready in time to accompany him. I try hard to match his long steps, and we talk as we cross the racecourse of things I've never spoken to anyone about before. I can see that he's an adult but his quiet intimate manner makes him seem more like a considerate older child. I wish the boys at school were like this. James Franklin never mentions football. Instead, he listens while I tell him of the ideas I used to have as I lay in bed as a small child. One morning, as we near the last gate across the tracks and he steps aside to let me through first, I ask him if he ever tried to think of nothingness. I tell him how difficult I used to find it because I always knew *I'd* be there – so the notion, to me, was a frustrating incongruity. The sound of horse's hooves and sulky's wheels spinning along behind us, down one of the tracks, makes us turn for a moment. He smiles at my question:

'Your problem is that you've been given no spiritual guidance, yet you have and *will* have many similar dilemmas in your life.'

We come to the road that runs alongside the station, and wait to cross. Beautiful James Franklin – the only man who's ever listened to what I say – puts a tentative hand under my elbow as we step off the kerb:

'I could attempt some answers for you – but I'm not sure your parents would like me for it.'

I think *he* sees me as a child. And paradoxically, out of everyone, I don't want him to. I watch him as he steps onto his train while I wait for mine. My mother lost a fiancé when she was very young. It's funny that I've never really thought before of how she must have felt. One morning, when my sister and I are fighting over who should practise the piano first, he comes into the room. My sister is planted firmly on the piano stool – sitting her ground. Her hands clench the edge of the seat – she's won again. I burst into tears of frustration and grief at my own impotence. I turn away to hide my wet face. A large white handkerchief appears over my shoulder. If I was infatuated yesterday, today the silent compassion of his gesture has cemented forever my loyalty and devotion. But he only stays for three months while he finishes his course. After that, our front bedroom houses a Lithuanian couple who speak no English. They use the kitchen from five o'clock to six in the evenings to concoct their extraordinary, aromatic fare. Our mother then prepares our meals from six o'clock onward, grumbling about the scraps of sauerkraut she finds on her stove. A few weeks ago I rode my bike to the Theology College and found out James Franklin's new address. But I never went to see him.

My little brother spends a lot of his time in his room these days. He has many collections. Badges from the war pinned onto a large square of black velvet. Tiny detailed lead soldiers carrying ammunition or rifles with fixed bayonets – some lying down firing guns, others in crouching positions with German helmets. He uses my easel in his room for his beautiful paintings of scenery and houses. The Truancy Officer came to see my mother a few months ago, because my brother was absent so often from Caulfield Central school. His reports say he is not concentrating on his work and he's no longer at the top of his class. He says he's going to be an artist when he grows up. Last year it was a professional cyclist. For months he'd been watching the local celebrity, Billy Guyatt who lives nearby, flash past on his custom-made racer. A straggle of small boys from Naroona Road formed a motley phalanx that trailed through the streets of Caulfield after their hero. And after them, trotted the neighbourhood dogs.

Occasionally now, we see our father as we set off for school in the mornings. He went to the Parks and Gardens section of the local council for a job. All they had as temporary work was a position for a garbage man, so he took that. He sits atop the rubbish as his colleagues do. Sometimes he waves to us with an old shoe or an empty bottle he's found among the mound of waste. The other men like him because he's so quiet and agreeable. They call him 'proffa' and he has an occasional drink with them at the Turf Club Hotel on Fridays.

20
THE SEMINAR

Today, my father sits in the front garden with a pile of books beside him. I look at the titles on their spines as I approach him, and I see that they're all the same. My mother planted a slip our neighbour gave her from the daisy bush next door when we moved to Caulfield. Now it flourishes in its sandy soil, spilling out over the grass and softening the edges of the concrete path. My father is nearby in the lee of the bush. He's cut a sort of cupola among the tall roses that were here when we came, and this provides a leafy summer-house for him. I have to part two of the prickly overhanging stems before I can see his face. It's the palest peppermint green. Not because he's ill anymore – but the leaves above tint the top of his hair and the bridge of his long nose. He seems very pleased to talk to me. I suppose it's because my mother's away working at the hospital so much these days:

'Come into my parlour, said the spider to the fly . . . what can I do for you on this pulchritudinous day?'

The word he's used is so obscure to me that, for once, I feel safe to reveal my ignorance of it. I sit beside him, pressing close to his chair to avoid the thorns in his miniature jungle:

'On this *what* day? Why are you reading so many books with the same name?'

He looks at me and smiles. 'Because it's so significant in its implications, I want to read it more than once!' He laughs at his own joke, as I do, and continues: 'No, I'm not reading! I'm annotating!'

He looks down at the page.

'This could interest you. Jock Reuben – remember you met him in Canberra? – well, he's written a very exciting critique of Russell's *Education and the Social Order*. Reuben feels that the structure of most educational systems, even so-called modern ones, suffer by comparison with those in the truly progressive countries – Sweden, Denmark. Think about that in relation to your own school, my dear. You might even like to browse through one of his books this afternoon.'

While he's been talking, I've inspected the spiral of a snail's shell that lies nearby, seemingly devoid of its small occupant. I turn it over gingerly with the tip of my finger, jumping back a little when two shiny, exploratory horns emerge. My father leans forward to look at the object of my interest:

'Listening seems to be becoming a dying art these days.'

But there's no hint of sarcasm or remonstrance in his good-natured voice and he continues:

'You see the shape of the shell? Perhaps you've studied the Archimedes curve at school?'

He's going to tell me about it – give me more information than I would ever want to know, or could understand, about the shell's shape. I must escape as gracefully – as tactfully as I can. I rise to my feet, my hair tangling in the thorny canopy overhead:

'God! I left the kettle on, I think. Can I bring you a cup? What will it be – black or white and would you like sugar?'

His taste seems to vary these days:

'Black and white striped thank you! And as to the dilemma of the sugar – sweets to the sweet: Farewell!'

He must want me to go. I wait for a little more information but there isn't any forthcoming from under the rosebush. So I'll have to guess about the sugar. When I return five minutes later, he must have heard my footsteps on the concrete path and the slap of the fly-door behind me, because his large hand appears through the bush. He takes the tea, pushing the stems with his other hand, to allow the cup's safe passage:

'I was saying before . . . I have several friends coming for a seminar to discuss this book. I've bought them all a copy. I'm going to phone them this evening. If they're free next weekend, it'll be then.'

I'm in the middle of a dream, when I wake to hear his voice. He's talking in the hall down from our bedroom. Since that morning, months ago, I've found myself alarmed at the sound of a voice raised in the silence of a sleeping household. I sit up and look at my clock. It's two-thirty. My father speaks again. I can tell he's on the phone because there are long gaps after each burst of his voice. I go to the door, feeling the fist of apprehension in my stomach. Is my mother alright? Because I must know, I cross the passage to her room. I see the huddle of her shape in bed and I put my ear close. She's breathing regularly – even snuffles and shifts her position as if sensing my presence. So I return quickly and continue to listen from my bed. I hear my father slightly indignant now:

'Of *course* I've got a clock . . . my dear fellow, some things in life just can't wait till morning . . . all I'm asking now is for your briefest assessment of Ragossnig's interpretation of the matter . . . well yes, I'm aware that some people are asleep but . . . yes, I'm sorry . . . by the way, I do hope that date will suit you.'

I hear then, quite distinctly, the words 'bourgeois bastard!' He must have cradled the receiver. Oh, no! He's dialling again. There's a very long silence. My sister says something indecipherable in her sleep. I pull the blankets around my head and, as I do so, I hear my father whistling softly through his teeth. As he comes down the passage, his notes have a determined – almost menacing – core. He hesitates at our bedroom door. I recognise the tune. It's 'Sleeper's Wake' by Bach – one of his favourites that he heard on the radio only last night. It's designed, I think, for my slumbering sister, with whom he shares so much. I can't stop a smile coming, even though I'm so tired.

He continues to the kitchen. Then there's the soft clink of a spoon in a cup and the familiar brief squirt of water into the kettle. At seven o'clock I'm woken again. My father's in the passage, his voice raised:

'Yes thank you, I would very much appreciate a call back when you've showered. In the meantime before you do so, I would urge you to read Schoenheimer's comments on . . . oh! I see . . . no . . . I understand . . .'

At breakfast, my father announces that his seminar will be a little smaller than he'd hoped. But that thirteen people have practically committed themselves and one or two are doubtfuls. He's going into the university to recruit from other faculties, anyone interested in the ideas of Bertrand Russell and the notion of the marriage between Art and Science.

On the evening of the seminar, it rains heavily. My mother's at a meeting in Carnegie. At a quarter to eight my father adjusts first, the angle of the books that lie on the dining table, then moves a Vegemite jar of pink jasmine a fraction of an inch to the left. He urges us not to go to bed but to join his friends for the evening:

'The reason I think you might benefit from tonight's experience, is that the book I've selected for discussion is, in my view, perhaps the most vital that's been written in the last twenty years. I believe it's going to be an extremely seminal . . . note, my darlings, the link – seminar, seminal – perhaps girls, you could look that up – a document that will inspire debate, even argument.'

Having begun by standing in front of us as we sit, in our best clothes, now he breaks away. Almost as though an urgent, unseen hand has beckoned. He strides to the window as he talks, then back to the sofa where we sit. I look at my little brother beside me without moving my head, and he glances away quickly, unable to hide his smile. Our father continues to walk – you could almost say he dashes – as he adds some words of caution:

'. . . if I could ask you not to interrupt in this evening's proceedings. I must warn you there will be a degree of controversy centred around some aspects of the text. Many of the friends I have here tonight hold opinions on this subject that are *diametrically* opposed to mine. Discussion will be lively. Now children, why should I invite people here tonight, you may ask, whom I know will provoke me . . . will perhaps even try to howl me down? The reason is very simple but important.'

I look across at my little brother who is taking one of the neatly stacked jotters and a pencil from the regiment on the table. He starts to draw the nose of an aeroplane.

My father is gesticulating now, his huge expressive hands spread, palms outward, as he continues to stride about the room, negotiating furniture. He rushes to check that the books he's chosen as cross-references are as he arranged them five minutes before. They lie open on the floor. Many have small pieces of paper as bookmarks:

'Now the reason for asking the dissenters? Truth can only be discovered by the process of getting to the kernel of such matters as those we'll discuss tonight. I want not only the reinforcement of like-minded individuals, but I welcome too, those who disagree – and have the courage to do so!'

I see that my brother has completed the fuselage of his little bi-plane and is proceeding to draw the deep shading created by the wing on the lower edge of the body. His tongue licks along his bottom lip as he concentrates. During a slight pause in my father's speech to us, the pencil scratches like a bird's claw. My father frowns, momentarily disconcerted, but his enthusiasm does not wane:

'This may surprise you children, but I've also invited tonight, my friend Herbert Norris from the truck. His presence will add a very important dimension to our discussion. There is an innocence in the lack of formal education, a great sense of wonder sometimes to be found in the untutored mind. He'll bring his own, his unique unclouded vision – *primal* vision, if you like, to our evening – as he has during our many illuminating talks on the truck. Modesty forbids me, my dears, from saying that he hangs on my every word, but the man knows how to *listen*! – one of the most important skills in communication as I'm sure you'll agree.'

Just as he glances at the clock for the third time in five minutes, there's a knock on the door. It's precisely eight o'clock. I jump up and stumble past the row of dining chairs. On the front porch stand two people. The one who speaks to me is short with dark oiled hair slicked back, showing comb tracks:

'G'day – the name's Wacka Norris.'

He looks like a friendly but anxious seal. He's wearing a long woollen overcoat – or more accurately he's in the process of removing it. He looks at me intently:

'Let me guess – you're the one does all the pitchers? This is the wife, Marge – your dad reckoned bring her if I like – hope it's okay by all.'

I feel relieved. I'd been expecting a formal academic greeting and a stiff exchange of words at the door.

With Wacka Norris and his wife seated and leafing through the book presented to them, my father begins to elucidate, for their benefit, Bertrand Russell's basic position on education, which inevitably, my father claims, spills over into the areas of moral philosophy, justice, even war and peace.

At five to nine I hear a car stop outside. I'm nearest the door so I start the journey through the chairs again. This time I see before me a tall man with glasses and a goatee beard. He's impeccably dressed in tweed jacket and corduroy trousers. He uncoils a soft blue scarf from around his neck and shakes his black umbrella vigorously before stepping inside. I'm suddenly aware of our rusted fly door and the sand-blasted panel, with the crack in it which was there when we came to live here. This is the poet my father's spoken about. As I usher him into our sitting room and my father starts his introductions, there are echoing footsteps on our concrete path, which become duller as someone outside mounts the small step and walks across the wooden porch. This time I see an old man with white hair. He's hunched at the front bedroom window, face pressed against the glass and hands cupped to the sides of his head. He starts a little as I step outside, and I notice he has a hearing aid:

'I'm Raoul Helgendorf – am I in the right place? There aren't the usual voices one hears . . .'

The fact that he now has an audience, albeit small, seems to rouse my father to fresh heights of enthusiasm. At one stage his voice escalates to such a frenzied pitch that I look up at him with momentary alarm:

'So Russell, in this respect, could well have been quite wrong!'

Professor Raoul Helgendorf who is in front of me, his book on the empty seat beside him, shifts in his chair. He appears to adjust his hearing aid. My father actually sits down then, but leaps up only seconds later:

'Before I elaborate further on the book, it may be useful to discuss, for a moment, the man himself. The Bertrand Russell I first read about many years ago. His early theories, for example, on the reasons for political affiliation. The conflict, for him, between Reason and Temperament. Doctor Pope and I have had occasion to disagree on this matter but I implore you, my dear fellow, to remain silent for a moment.'

He looks across laughing, at Dr Pope, who sits attentive but stony-faced, with no apparent intention of interrupting. I feel uneasy. Then my father continues:

'I can go back over these remarks when the others arrive,' he glances at his watch, 'but I don't think we can keep you waiting any longer. Now, I have a few notes here that are discussion starters – the preliminary dissertation, if you will.'

While my father talks, I watch my brother complete the details of his picture on the jotting pad. The aeroplane he's drawn with such exacting attention to its authenticity, flies past clouds and over the tops of a row of dark, minutely-detailed, winter-naked trees. Behind them is a full, florin moon with a lightly sketched suggestion of features. I hear my father mention the name of Carl Jung and I listen for a moment:

'So you may feel that Jung and Russell would, in some respects, make strange bedfellows – so much at variance are many of their ideas. For example, Russell struggles with the notion of faith versus proof, whereas Jung's religious convictions, though not strictly orthodox in some respects, are quite unquestioned in his own philosophy.'

My brother is adding something to his page. I find myself leaning forward so that I can see across his arm. He's drawing what looks like a cat at first but suddenly, as he pencils in ears and tail, I recognise that it's a dog of some sort, or a wolf. Its mouth is a small black 'O' as it howls, head raised toward the moon. Then my brother adds a speech bubble from the wolf's mouth. And the single word 'Ra-oull' inside it. I'm quite incapable of holding back a strangled yelp of laughter and my father looks quickly across, surprised and gratified at my keen interest and apparent concurrence with what he's saying. My sister, who's been listening to him all this time, even straining forward in her seat to show her involvement, sees the picture of the wolf. We hastily leave the room, knocking two empty chairs, whose backs smash together like a rifle shot. We have to run the length of the hall, through the kitchen and out to the back garden, before we can release our suffocating hysteria. Ten minutes later, having splashed our faces over the kitchen sink and tucked handkerchiefs up our sleeves, we return to the room, eyes averted from our brother and his drawing.

My father is standing on a chair that he's taken to the window. His voice is raised to a shout. Then he stops to pin sheets of paper to the curtain which has become a makeshift blackboard. In the awful silence of the room, the others sit looking up at him:

'Now, perhaps if I could ask you to take each of these points in sequence ... and *note* – though they may make a strange-looking design, I've placed them quite significantly, I think you'll agree.'

He stands on tiptoe and the chair teeters. Wacka Norris rushes forward to steady it, and my father hitches the rings across the rod, fractionally, so that his pinned papers don't bulge forward as much. He sounds triumphant now:

'Why have I used a different colour for each of the headings for his theses? The reasons will emerge.'

The cat that slept fitfully before, on the sofa next to my brother, now leaps to the floor. It crouches by the door to the hall. Dr Pope waits for a gap in my father's excited monologue:

'I'm afraid I promised to be home early. Perhaps you could post your – notes – so I can peruse them at my leisure.'

His hand is on the embossed metal knob of the door. My father turns. His hair is awry. His face flushed. He has a sheet of paper in one hand. He seems crestfallen for a moment. Then he jumps down. As Dr Pope opens the door, the cat slinks quickly through. My father returns as his colleague's footsteps recede down the front path. He takes up his position in front of his diminished audience:

'Now, my friends! I invite discussion!'

There's silence like a deep, dark well. I feel so anxious for my father. I wish I could think of something. I can hear the clock. It seems to be ticking on forever. Then kind, sweet, Wacka Norris stands. His jumper cuffs are rolled back and his trousers are two or three inches clear of his shoes. They reveal maroon socks with a small darn and a little yellow clock on the ankle:

'Well, proffa, I agree with that feller, Young, you were saying about before. Like – there's a family lives down the street from me and Marge. They're that religious – always at church and that. But religion hasn't been conductive to *them* being happy. The wife's always yelling abuse and her old man hits the bottle. Like, we had the Religious Instruction at school of a Friday . . .'

My father breaks in:

'Excellent point, Wacka, you've really hit the nail there. As Jung says – religion can so easily be perverted into a form of blackmail. I'm not a religious man myself – I imagine if I were more interested, I'd probably prefer, perhaps, a pantheistic approach to the subject . . .'

Rain, which has been drizzling sporadically all evening, now pours down in earnest. There's a flick of lightning and I see in the gap between the curtains, our front garden, clear as a summer's day – a spectacular flashlight snap-shot, that captures for me tall roses, the white island of daisies, and the matchstick fence. Then it's gone. Thunder follows, rolling and

163

billowing away across the suburbs.

It's five minutes past ten. Raoul Helgendorf rises and extends his hand:

'I find your ideas – er – refreshing – but I'll have to call myself a cab if I may and leave you all. When you get to my age . . . '

My father seems undeterred by his friend's relatively precipitate departure. I watch Wacka Norris. He seems uneasy now with responsibililty for all future reaction, his alone. But he and his wife stay politely attentive for ten more minutes and, during a gap in my father's dialogue, they excuse themselves. Momentarily a little subdued, my father opens his copy of the book and leafs through it:

'Ahead of its time, of course, children – people just aren't prepared to relinquish their preconceived notions about such subjects. A pity they left. I so much wanted to discuss a matter of crucial significance. Namely, the marriage of Art and Science. But perhaps such a subject would warrant a separate seminar.'

We help our father tidy the room. My sister goes quickly to the seats first vacated by the visitors, takes the books that lie on each of the two chairs, and places them with the stack already on the table.

21
THROUGH SUNGLASSES DARKLY

I've cut myself a fringe. It hangs to my eyebrows and it's crooked. I don't think it suits my face too well, but somehow it gives me a sense of comfort. My father refers to me as Greta Garbo and makes jokes about my wanting to be alone. When I told him I didn't want to *want* to be alone he just said:

'Here's a sentence with even more repetition of the same word – let me see if I can get it right – "Arthur, whereas Ann had had 'had', had had 'had had'. Had 'had had' had the examiner's approval, Ann would have passed." '

The difference between us was that I was serious and he wasn't.

My friend Bernadette Shannon doesn't come to visit any more. I think it's partly because of my father but I can't feel angry with him because he loves visitors so much. He left the University six weeks ago. The last time Bernadette Shannon came he took her aside to show her the book he was studying at the time. It was *The Critique of Pure Reason* by Immanuel Kant and she remained totally silent for an hour while he explained its theories. I sat there feeling uncomfortable and trying to think of ways to extract my friend from my father's room. Actually, it isn't difficult to sidetrack him these days, but unfortunately he has a new habit of connecting everything you say, even if you've deliberately changed the subject. So deflecting him can lead to worse excesses than those you're trying to avoid. He's made quite a hobby of doing this. My mother calls it an obsession. So I waited for Bernadette Shannon that day, my new fringe tickling my face till it itched, and the sunglasses I bought after I'd cut my hair resting unaccustomedly on my nose. When my friend said goodbye at the gate after a short game of Monopoly, I felt a gap between us where there hadn't been one before, and she didn't look back and wave.

My father says only film stars wear dark glasses when it's not sunny. But he wore them himself one Saturday morning at breakfast. And seemed to enjoy doing it, as it gave him an opportunity for one of his quotes. While my mother read the *Age* and smoked a cigarette, he sat at the table buttering his toast:

'*Now we see through a glass darkly . . .* '

Noting our confusion, he tried to elucidate:

'St Paul, my little ignorami . . . he's talking about reality and how we understand only what we perceive.'

My sister will be seventeen in June of next year. She wants to go to Melbourne University to do an arts course so she can be a social worker. My big brother joined the air force three years ago, just before we came to Melbourne. Occasionally he's able to send a little money to help. But he never puts his address. We know from the postmark that he's in a country centre in Victoria. My father's job on the truck has finished and he modelled some clothes for a photographer called Helmut Newton last week. But his job as a model is not permanent. There's my mother's hospital wages and a little help from the government, but my sister must get some sort of work so she can save for her university fees. There's a theatre near Caulfield station that has a candy bar. She prepares and serves drinks during the interval, then washes glasses till the film is over. After that she mops the floor of the confectionery area and at eleven-thirty she rides her bike home across the dark racecourse.

On Saturday mornings, dressed as twins in our high school summer dresses, we walk up Naroona Road and along the main street near the railway gates to Rowlands drapery. We sell haberdashery from nine o'clock till twelve when the shop closes.

My sister read an advertisement for sales girls in the paper. When she answered it, she found that a photographer takes pictures of people's houses in Caulfield and mounts them on the fronts of calendars. So my sister's task is to sell these from door to door. The pictures are what the photographer describes as 'the quality homes' and the way the photos are processed is 'artistic'. They have a misty effect around the edge. On the first day my sister is to start her round down in Glen Eira Road, she brings home her wares to show us. We see views of houses taken mostly from well below eye level. Balconies bulge. Curved windows glint in the sun, with ruched, ecru curtains behind – the current fashion for such houses. Gardens are geometrically neat as though the owner takes a ruler and set square with him, as well as his fork and spade. And the hedges! Most are clipped neatly with shoe-box-accurate right angles, but some are rich with the skill of the amateur topiarist. One even has an elephant with two smaller ones following.

We sit eating a lunch of tinned vegetable soup which my mother's extended by adding milk and flour. I see how tired she looks. Her hair is more grey than black now, and she wears glasses for reading. She attributes that fact to the French Flowers which she says ruined her eyesight. She's bought herself a yellow and black book titled *Teach Yourself Typing* and every morning, if she's not working, she must, according to the rules, type an entire page of the *Age*. She says she has more chance of getting a better job if she learns this skill. Also it will help because one day she wants to write a book. I sit looking at her. Or rather I watch the parts of her face I can see through the blue vase of misty Baby's Breath between us. She bought the seeds last year and planted them against the fence at the back near the fig tree. She's put, with the fragile flowerlets, some frilled-edge Boston fern that grows along the dark moist path by our house. I saw my brother and his friend, Alan Patterson, smoking cigarettes down there last week. Opposite me, the drift from her De Reszke lies like a long, blue cirrus above our heads. In one way my parents' roles are changed these days. Even my mother's loud voice is eclipsed by my father's phrenetic enthusiasm. She goes to bed earlier than she did before she worked so hard. And although she's only forty-seven, sometimes her head falls against her chest in sleep when she's reading outside, protected by her garden screen. I notice that my father's finished his soup. He wipes his mouth with his napkin:

'Today I feel lucky. When the people have bought their calendars they may be well-disposed enough to hire a gardener to perpetuate the perfection of their showpieces. I could have twenty customers by the end of today!'

He turns to my sister:

'I'll make up some cards before you set off.'

My mother sighs, butts her cigarette and puts her hand on his arm for a moment:

'Do calm down. You're getting over-excited again. Go to the department of Parks and Gardens on Monday and try for another regular gardening job.'

My father suddenly smashes his fist onto the table. The pepper and salt containers jump, and the Baby's Breath quivers in its vase:

'I don't *want* to calm down. I don't like feeling sad and dead – or rather, not feeling at all! If you must know, the only thing I feel at this moment, apart from anger at all of you for not understanding, is a sensation that I'm on the brink of a precipice.'

I can feel my face flush with fear and confusion. My father has never been angry before. Not really angry. I lift the egg cup of salt and put it back where it was before. I notice that it's spilled some of its fine particles. They remain on the table, leaving a clear circle with the small graduated fall of salt around it. My little brother runs from the room. I hear his bedroom door close. My sister looks frightened. Her eyes are on my father, as she says quietly:

'Daddy we *do* understand . . . even about the precipice . . .'

Her voice trails away. She looks at me then at our mother who, for once, appears devoid of a response:

'I could ask anyone who seems nice, if they need a regular gardener.'

My father's in bed again. My mother doesn't say anything about flu this time. In fact, she doesn't mention his illness at all. She takes him his meals on a tray, and reads him the papers in the mornings before she goes to work in the hospital. I notice his little bedside table holds books and his pipe and often a thermos, but no chemist's bottles. Every Wednesday my mother goes with him into town to see a doctor in Collins Street. Sometimes when I wake in the night or can't sleep, I go to his room to look at him. My sister does too, because occasionally when I wake, I see in the half-light her blankets pulled back and her bed empty. Then I watch her return in her nightie.

I've been wearing the dark glasses for five weeks now. I only take them off at school and when I go to bed. In a sense, I feel distinguished – at least there's something *about* me now, but I'm aware that my mother seems uneasy, almost annoyed. Sometimes she comes over and removes them when I've sat down to eat. And I feel the strangest sense of being naked at those times. I think my sister's sarcasm about the glasses stems from her jealousy. I do get a lot of attention and comment that I never had before.

One day my mother tells me that I'll have to miss a morning's school; that she's made an appointment to take me to an office in the Manchester Unity Building in the city, where you do Vocational Guidance Tests. It's on the fourth floor and we travel in a tiny lift with a fancy concertinaed iron gate that shuts with a bang after you've stepped inside. It's strange and new being so confined, so close to my mother. I can smell the powder she puts on her face when she comes to town. And the familiar leather scent of her old, soft bag. When you look upward there's a dreadful feeling of panic as you watch the moving black cables that control the ascent of the lift. I have a fantasy, as we rise higher, of cutting the licorice-like ropes with my father's shears. Either I'd be electrocuted in the process, if there's wiring underneath, or our small carriage would hurtle downward, our hair standing on end and our necks feeling the unfamiliar wind. I stand there, imagining vividly the impact through my feet and body as we hit the concrete basement. There are fence-like sides here in the lift. Metal – like the gate that clanged shut on the ground floor, and I can see each subsequent level going past as we get closer to the fourth floor. Once, the lift stops between levels and I think my final hour has come. I can feel sweat trickling all over me, as if a myriad flies are wandering under my clothes. I glance at my mother through my dark glasses. She stands, eyes calm and looking straight ahead, holding her bag in front of her with gloved hands. When I step up, because we've stopped three or four inches down from the fourth level, I feel such relief that I'm actually looking forward to doing the tests. At least they won't be life-threatening like the lift.

We walk down narrow green corridors and listen to our footsteps behind us on the linoleum. It's dark and there are occasional high transom windows that are reinforced with wire. My mother comments on how far we've had to walk and her voice, a loud whisper today because of the proximity of the shiny walls, reverberates around us. Finally we come to a door that's open. A young woman in a short white coat, like a doctor's, comes from behind a desk and extends her hand to my mother. She asks me my name and tells me she's a psychologist. I have to go into another cubicle to do my tests. I can hear the two women talking – but nothing of what they're saying. Their voices become one with the faint sound of traffic below in Swanston Street. At one point, the psychologist comes in and touches my shoulder:

'It might be easier for you without the glasses, but there aren't any actual rules about them, so leave them on if you'd like to.'

I take them off and certainly the figures, geometrical shapes and printing, are clearer. I answer a sheet of questions about what sorts of books I prefer to read. Then I look at some large black splodges that have twin images connected to them. I have to write down anything they remind me of. After an hour, I return to the room where my mother sits talking – in time to hear her say:

'My poor husband's illness has disrupted the whole

household.'

The psychologist indicates a chair for me to sit on beside my mother. She smiles at me over her desk:

'I was going to come and get you soon, but sit down. I'll go and bring your papers.'

She's gone for ten minutes. My mother looks at me:

'Probably having a cuppa.'

Because she's whispering, she has to imitate someone tilting a cup to their lips and holding a saucer. I don't really know why I'm here, but I feel relief that I've done the tests. I look at her through my sunglasses:

'And a pink cake in a pleated paper cup. With pale pink icing, and a little silver ball on the summit.'

My mother smiles, showing her dimples:

'And pâté and asparagus sandwiches with relish spread . . . ssh!'

We hear footsteps. The psychologist sits across her desk now and looks down as she shuffles papers. Then she reaches for a pen and turns to me:

'You lived in Canberra for three years. That must have been interesting?'

Although she's looking at me, it's my mother who replies:

'She liked the high school. But what a place! If it's not almost snowing in Canberra, the sun's so hot and the flies so bad you have to wear hats and protective veils.'

The psychologist rises slightly, tilts her chair so she faces me directly, and sits again. There's a silence. She hasn't moved her eyes from my face. She's so pretty. When she smiles at me I notice you can see only her bottom teeth. Not the top ones:

'So you really liked the high school in Canberra?'

My mother's breath, drawn in sharply to start speaking, causes the psychologist to raise her hand, just slightly, toward my mother. I want to talk about our house in Acton Road, the daily ride on my bike through the leafy avenue to school, but I don't know if that's what I'm supposed to say. I look down at a knot in the wood on the edge of the desk and the wavy streaks of the grain surrounding it:

'Yes, I liked the high school.'

She leans toward me, staring at my hidden eyes:

'Have you ever noticed how it's difficult to talk to someone when you can't see their eyes? You can read so much from the expression in them. Mouths say the words but eyes show the feelings.'

'I haven't thought about that.'

She moves a little in her chair and clasps her hands on the desk. After a moment she speaks very softly:

'Which do you think it is? With the glasses on, the world can't see how you feel? Or *you* can't see the world so clearly . . . and its troubles?'

'I don't know.'

I have a constricted feeling in my throat and my eyes are hot cinders.

'Would you be prepared to take them off for a minute? Then describe to me how you feel just at that moment? Then you could put them back.'

'I don't know.'

Silence reaches to the walls, ceiling and floor:

'Would it be any easier if your mother went out?'

'I don't know.'

I'm looking at my shoes. I listen to my mother's chair as it scrapes over the linoleum, and her feet – her dear tired feet – as they take her through the door. I hear the psychologist lean back in her chair. Her voice is further away than before:

'Now.'

I remove my dark glasses. I can't look at her because she'll see the tears that I'm trying to swallow back. Trying very hard. But not succeeding. They won't stop. They're running from my eyes and trickling down my nose. I look at the painting behind her head. It shows a mother holding a baby very close. There's a window in the background of the picture and you can see just a single tree, a beautifully painted tree, through it. She hands me a little folded ironed handkerchief with a blue and green rose embroidered in one corner:

'What do you see in the painting?'

'I see a lovely tree.'

'And no people?'

'Oh yes, I see the mother and baby – but I was looking at the tree.'

'Have you thought what you'd like to be when you've grown up?'

'I'd like to be an artist but you can't make a living. So I'll be training as a mothercraft nurse because I love babies.'

I'm able to look at her now. As she writes, I wipe my face. She looks up from her notes:

'You could do anything you like, as long as it doesn't involve maths.'

Now I don't know what to do with the hanky. It's a sodden ball. I turn my hand over, knuckles upward on my lap so she won't see it and be reminded of the shame of my tears. I think she must have noticed because she says with a laugh:

'Keep the hanky, I get hundreds every Christmas. I've spoken to your mother about talking to you again.'

My mother and I return in the lift. It's much better going down. You don't have that feeling of panic. I suppose it's because the further you descend, the less space there is to fall if the cables *do* break. We reach the bottom and pull back the squeaky metal gateway to step through. Swanston Street is crowded with shoppers. The light is incredibly glary in contrast to inside. My mother suggests lunch at Myer's cafeteria. I reach over and kiss her thin cheek. I put my sunglasses back on and we move together into the mass of people.

22
REFLECTIONS

My sister's job selling calendars has finished. Now she works after school at the blood bank of the Royal Melbourne Hospital next to University High School. One evening, she comes rushing up the path and bursts through the door. She drops her school bag and stands waiting to catch her breath:

'Remember I was asked to go to the country with the mobile unit today after lunch? Well, guess – just *guess* who I saw? Quickly, *quickly* – I can't *wait* to tell you!'

We've been eating our dinner. My mother swallows her mouthful in one large gulp, leaving a speck of shepherd's pie on the corner of her mouth. She dabs at it with her table napkin:

'It sounds as though you saw Jesus Christ himself.'

'I practically *did*! That's how I felt! I can't wait, I'll just *have* to tell you! There he was, lying down with his eyes shut so that at first I didn't realize it was him. One of his arms was stretched out . . .'

My mother interrupts:

'It's sounding more and more like Jesus Christ – go on!'

'It was our beautiful, our incomparable, our long lost brother!'

My little brother stops eating and my mother looks up:

'Good Lord, what next! How is he?'

'He's well. But you'll never guess this part – he's *married*!'

My sister tells us that he didn't recognise her until she'd sat down beside him in the Nissen hut which served as a temporary ward. She was starting to swab his arm, when he'd swivelled his head round and looked closely at her in her white uniform and said:

'Hello little blister!'

My mother leaves to bring the plate of dinner that she's keeping warm. As my sister starts eating, she tells us that she'd found someone to take over while she sat and talked to our brother for half an hour. She says he's been married for ten months and his wife is eighteen and has blonde hair. He's based at Laverton. He's only been there for a year. Before that he was stationed on Manus Island. They live with his wife's sister in Alamein. He's saving up to buy one of the new Holden cars. My mother breaks in:

'"Australia's Own Car", indeed! Designed in Detroit – an adaptation of a Chevrolet – it's all part of the insidious Yankee colonisation.'

My father comes to the door, a gaunt figure in a checked dressing gown. He stands there, tying a glossy emerald-green cord. Its brilliant tassles wobble as he knots it. The cat got the old one last week, and we keep finding shreds of silk under chairs. He finishes slowly and deliberately securing the bow, and moves it across a little so it's exactly in the centre of the dressing gown:

'Have I missed some news?'

My sister's knife and fork clatter onto her plate as she repeats her story. My father stands a moment longer, then says in a slow thick voice as he turns to go:

'Perhaps he'll come to see us.' And seems moved to add: 'That would be so nice.'

Our brother visits us three weeks later, bringing with him his shy little bride. His skin is tanned and he looks like the fuzzy-wuzzy angels we talked about during the war. He's grown taller – as big, in fact, as my father. His curly hair has darkened. He rolls up his sleeves for my little brother to feel his hard muscles. My sister and I can't take our eyes off him. It's difficult for me to equate the boy I last saw – a diffident and gangling adolescent – with this self-possessed young man who seems so articulate. We touch him again and again to make sure he's real, and he laughs self-deprecatingly. You can see that he's relieved to have returned; that it's taken some courage to come back. My mother shows great interest in his wife, encouraging her to talk about the life she led before she met our brother. She spent her childhood in a small house in Collingwood. Her life had been one of deprivation and illness. She was brought up by a stepmother. Her brother served in the airforce and lived on Manus Island at the same time as ours. She was introduced to our brother by letter and the two corresponded for several months, before they married on our brother's return to Australia.

We sit in the garden on our old silvery-grey bench of plaited wood, and the cat plays among fallen virgilea blossoms. My father even leaves his bed for an hour, and brings a deck chair from the wash house to listen. My brother and his wife start their walk to the station at five o'clock. The three of us stand on the footpath and watch them till they turn the corner at the end of Naroona Road. He says he'll come back soon, but I don't know that he will. His life is different now.

I've started going to art classes every Friday night. You don't have tuition, so it's more just a group than a class. The studio belongs to a famous sculptor called Ola Cohn, who studied with Henry Moore. I heard about it from a friend of my mother's. You have to be invited to join, so my mother posted some of my pictures to Ola Cohn, who sent a welcoming letter back. She's a large distinguished-looking woman who covers her lack of contours with a voluminous blue smock, secured at the front with a big ruby brooch. Her hair is dark grey and it's wound round to the nape of her neck in a thick bun. She has compassionate dark eyes set like raisins in her fleshy face. And an air of authority – of confidence. She believes in fairies and elves. I like her immediately.

She lives in East Melbourne in a two-storeyed house. Well, the bottom storey was a coach-house long ago and is now the studio, and you walk up a treacherously uneven flagstoned drive to reach it. It's more a courtyard than a drive, as the building is L-shaped and set a long way back from the road. There are old tangled trees on either side of the wide path. Their leaves touch overhead like a maze of black scribble. You can hardly see the house until you're almost at its door. Ola Cohn's pieces of dull, bronze sculpture lie gracefully among the violas and sweet alyssum that grow between the humps of the flagstones. And there are terracotta busts of children – some on tree trunk pedestals in the garden. There's always the strong smell of woodsmoke and coal that she burns in the studio's open fire. It fills the courtyard and the air is heavy with it as you walk down Gipps Street from the bus. On Saturday mornings, I can smell it in my hair from the night before. She has so many cats I can't count them. Some curl up on the artists' laps as they work. Others stretch out on the warm bricks of the hearth, their fur shiny in the firelight. There's a magpie too. It doesn't live in a cage but walks impudently among the artists and whistles its extraordinary songs. I find its blackness and boldness quite terrifying and, when it cocks its head at me, I shy away from its uncompromising eye.

Ola Cohn married late in her life and lives in the upper level over the studio with her husband Mr Green. There's a very steep flight of wooden steps to reach it. When you look up there from the courtyard, you see the edges of the slate roof and below that the picturesque multi-paned windows of her small kitchen. The sills are a prodigious mass of coral geraniums that she's planted up there in boxes. One Friday evening I arrive early. She sees me from her window and leans out, elbows deep in flowers, to call me upstairs:

'Come up – I want to see you for a minute.'

I sit on a patchwork cushion on the floor, and we talk till the others arrive. She has brass ornaments in her shady sitting room, that reflect the windows and all the colours and shapes. She's put one – it looks like a large jug or vase – on a bookshelf near the small fire where I sit. The body of it is almost spherical and narrows to a graceful neck with a handle on one side. On its rounded cheek, I can see the whole of Ola Cohn's room compressed into one small cameo in which the walls are bowed and elongated. All the pieces of sculpture, the paintings and velvet-covered chairs, are mirrored on the jug, in variations of its curve. A wall rug in subdued tones that hangs in reality on my left, becomes a multi-hued panorama behind my head. Ola Cohn leaves to make a pot of tea. I reach out to touch the glowing ornament, and my hand becomes a giant's, obscuring all that's behind it. I sit back, my eyes still on the jug: Its replica room, with the brightest spot the spangle of the window, fascinates me. Ola Cohn returns with the tray of tea. She puts it on a large corduroy footstool, sits down , and reaches into the pocket of her blue smock. I'm confused when she hands me a piece of folded paper. Is it a bill because I've been in the group? I don't know what to do, so I hold it in one hand, my tea in the other, thinking that to be the most sophisticated course of action. We drink in silence. Then she places her empty cup beside her, where it almost disappears in the folds of her dress:

'Aren't you going to see what it is I've given you?'

I read what she's written – at least, I read the part that seems to jump out at me from the page:

'Therefore I recommend that my pupil be accepted at the appropriate age for study at the National Gallery Art School.'

I leave the group at nine o'clock that night, catching the early bus. I give my mother the precious letter to read. She seems to be taking a long time, but perhaps I'm impatient for her reaction. She stands up to hug me and kisses me on top of my head. Then we take the letter to my father's bedroom.

I expect to see him lying in his customary position under the blankets, but this time he's sitting on the side of the bed surrounded by cuttings from the newspaper. My mother hands him my reference. When he's finished reading it, his arm encircles my neck and he presses his head against mine:

'I'll write to my cousin Hal in New Zealand tomorrow – the whole clan will know quickly that way.'

Neither of them says anything, but I know that unless things change, I can't go. The fees are prohibitive and art isn't a career anyway. I'm aware that they can barely keep me as it is. It's the honour that we're celebrating as my mother brings tea and the chocolate biscuits that she's been saving for such an occasion.

We sit and I tell them about the little high room with the geraniums at the window and the brass jug. My father's so happy tonight. He says all his cousins are artists and poets in New Zealand. Long after I've gone to bed, the piece of paper under my pillow, I hear him telephoning and wandering up and down the passage. At two o'clock in the morning he opens the front door, and ten minutes later I hear the whisper of his footsteps through the ferns as he walks down the side of the house just below my window. He's whistling 'Anna Magdalena' under his breath.

Our Lithuanian boarders left a few weeks ago and my sister and I have our old bedroom back. The house is the way it used to be when we moved in, but with one difference. My father has taken over the sitting room for some important research he's doing, so we have to sit in the dining room after dinner at night. We've pushed the table and chairs up against the wall and my father's given us the sofa and the radio. Occasionally he brings home people he used to know from the university. He doesn't want his research papers disturbed, so he and his friends sit in his bedroom. My father does most of the talking. He leaves the door open, since it's October and the evenings are warm. You can hear his conversations from our bedroom across the passage. Last night my father's voice was raised to such a pitch that my sister and I stopped talking to listen:

' . . . but this is the whole problem of philosophy, my dear chap . . . physical representations of intellectual concepts. In astronomy, for example, they've made actual structures of the solar system . . . in physics a model can be built of a Cartesian diver, to demonstrate air pressure.'

I've just started to tap out a song for my sister. We use our knuckles on the sides of the dressing-table, rapping out the first two lines and the other has to guess the rest. I hear my father's voice raised again and something he's saying – and the way he's emphasising it interests me. I'm only as far as: *In Dublin's fair city, where the maids are so pretty . . .*

I think he must have walked to the door. His voice is suddenly clearer:

'But you see in dealing with the mind – its complexity, perhaps its nature, is such that there's been no solid *con*struct . . .'

I thought my father would be discussing the unconscious part of the mind. His preamble had seemed in some way to indicate this. I can imagine now, his hands sweeping the air to add weight to his words. And his friend perhaps levering himself from his chair in an attempt to go because it's getting late. I was probably right because my father says:

'Please allow me to continue. It's most important. It was a long, long time before man turned his attention to the mind itself, to its mechanics. Though I can see attempts were made . . . but with little real impact or, shall we say, success in furthering the understanding of human motivation. At the turn of the century, Freud, Jung, et al, were not building a physical *construct* but rather postulating theories in purely intellectual terms to explain human behaviour. So if we could build a model in which it were possible to understand thought processes . . . if we could attempt to witness the actual workings of the human mind . . . just think, my dear fellow, just imagine the ramifications of *that*!'

I look at my clock. It's eleven-thirty. I turn on my side to prepare for sleep. Tomorrow is a school day.

23
THE DOG'S BREAKFAST

The porch is damp this evening but I like to sit and smell the garden after rain. Anyway the sun's out again and because it's December, you can just detect faint steam rising from the boards. Sometimes you see things that make your heart turn over. Like a sparrow bathing in a puddle – and the blur of its tiny wings. I breathe in the moist aftermath air and I can taste the rain-smell in the back of my mouth. The leaves are still beaded, and they hang lower than before. I know, because I often sit here these days and from this position you can see that the foliage of the plane tree on our nature-strip just clears the racecourse wall across the road. Whereas today, its heavy leaves obscure the first few inches. The sitting room where my father is doing his research, is nearby – just inside the front door to the right. I can hear noises in there and occasionally a hummed phrase or two of Bach or Scarlatti, or a piece from my sister's *Sonatina* book.

Last week the sounds of dragged furniture were so puzzling that I went around the front of the house to look through the windows. But he'd drawn the curtains. Our mother caught a glimpse of his work in there while gardening a few weeks ago, before he'd closed them. When we asked her what the research project was about, she'd laughed with a sort of bitterness:

'Research! It looks more like a dog's breakfast than a study.'

He works in there most nights and sometimes during the day and he always locks the door behind him whether he's going in or coming out. Our mother says at least his preoccupations keep him out of mischief. Last month a young constable brought him home. My father had been up in Glenhuntly Road in his pyjamas. He tried to engage the policeman in a conversation in the dining room about Marxism. When that didn't work, my father presented him with a crisp sheet of paper and a sharpened pencil and invited him to enumerate the reasons for pyjamas being indecent or offensive in the street but not in the house. The policeman called my father 'matey' and 'chief', and seemed very friendly. He told him that he was letting him off with a warning. I think about my father as I sit watching the birds that now dot the lawn looking for worms, and I listen to the trickle of water still coming from the down-pipes.

My father's grown a small grey – almost white – goatee beard and he wears a black beret. Although he looks handsome, I don't like all the changes, and the beard seems symbolic of them. Synonymous with the way he doesn't listen seriously to what you say any more but makes strange, obscure jokes in response. For example, yesterday I was drawing a map for school and wanted to borrow a blue pencil because I'd mislaid mine. I went to his bedroom door to ask. He was sitting on the floor in his new bright yellow shirt with papers in a circle around him. Like the yolk of an egg surrounded by its white:

'A blue pencil? Ah! The feminine ethos emerges already!' he'd replied. 'At the tender age of fifteen she wishes to *restrict*! A new dampening influence is about to descend on our household! No more shall the free flow of ideas have uninterrupted passage! No more shall we stroll with Boccaccio through the baroque by-ways of *The Decameron*!'

He'd caught me looking at him, dumbstruck:

'Clottus ineptus! You don't follow? String! Cerebral string! ... so necessary for connecting one concept to another, my dear. Don't you see? You want a blue pencil . . . you want to perpetuate the timeless inclinations of your sex and use that pencil to censor what goes on in my head!'

Áll I'd wanted was the colour for the sea round the perimeter of my map.

My mother is restive. We've been excluded from the sitting room for several weeks now. She remarks on the lack of adequate lighting in the dining room for her sewing and reading in the evenings. There's nowhere quiet for us to do our homework and she can't have any discussion groups at night any more. And she's concerned at our father's constant activities that have prevented him from eating and sleeping properly. She says that whenever she wakes at night, she can hear him moving about in the sitting room or walking the passage and the paths outside. Today, at lunch, her patience is at an end. My father, whom she has persuaded to join us, takes a minute piece of lamb's fry on the end of his fork and responds to her tirade:

'Mundane considerations like yours are preventing the world's progress! Can't you distinguish the pedestrian from the significant? Matters such as routine – eating, sleeping etcetera *dominate* this household! My project is almost complete, please be patient if you will!'

It's December the tenth 1950. My father appears at breakfast in a shining red party hat with thin crepe paper streamers falling from its apex. He wears the slender white elastic, not under his chin in customary fashion, but below his bottom lip as soldiers do in diggers' hats. He rises from his seat and puts his hand to the side of his forehead in a salute:

'My darlings, the battle between your mother and me is over. I wave the white flag. Follow me please.'

My father's project in the sitting room is ready for us to view. At last, after so long, we are permitted entry. He opens the door like a showman drawing aside glittering curtains. With a flourish, he ushers the four of us in. My mother steps quickly forward and glances around. She turns and moves to block my little brother's progress. But he ducks under her arm. I take a small step and stand just inside the doorway. The room is shaded – my father has kept the curtains together. Footprints, shaped from newspaper, lead from the door to what appears to be a sort of altar. A stack of books reaches almost to the ceiling. On top of them is our kitchen tray and propped upright on it a large framed photograph of my sister. At its sides, on the tray, two candles flicker brightly in the shaded room. My father has pencilled a moustache on my sister's face. String, tied to the frame of the picture, connects to the handle of a kettle. This rests on a pile of bricks to the left. Still further toward the window is a dining chair. On it lies a torch whose beam illuminates the photograph of my father's younger brother James, who was killed in action in World War One, aged twenty. His medals adorn the thick wooden frame. Beside the chair lie his foxed letters from the Front. And next to those, a loaf of bread. To the right of my sister's towertop photo, there's a table with a picture of our mother in an oval frame. And alongside, others of my two brothers and my sister and me. A hammer holds down copies of the *Guardian* newspaper. And a clock ticks loud seconds away as we stand perusing the outcome of our father's industry. Tied to the leg of the table with string, there's a row of cardboard cylinders of various heights and next to that, on the right, a mountain of clothing with a large notice secured with a safety pin. Without stepping forward, I peer across to read its message: 'The mountain is both the obstacle and the way'. Empty jam tins with ragged lids stand upright among the bottom layer of clothes. My father has glued a sort of frieze around the walls far above. I look up to read part of its legend. 'Never send to know for whom the bell tolls. It tolls for thee.'

I try to find meaning in my father's construction. Oh, all the items are familiar – the components, that is. But the rationale, if there is one, is not immediately obvious.

My father stands tremblingly aside and waits for the impact of his creation to prompt some reaction. I look at my mother and see that she's taking my brother's hand. My father can't contain himself. He starts shouting excitedly and I soon realise that this is no random display:

'You notice the string? In our minds, events and thoughts are seldom disconnected! The bread is the very staff of life. Life and death – as close as laughter and tears. Tears – my brother James. The bricks? Something from outside that is now inside. Events occur outside and our reactions to those happenings are inside!

You notice the frieze? "Never send to know for whom the bell tolls . . . " Donne, like Carl Jung, knew that when it tolls for one of us, it tolls for all. And the clock? Time also, my dears, is of the essence. Here's Donne's concept of time encapsulated . . . '

He looks up again at the wall, finds the words he wants and reads:

' "Time, which rots all and makes botches poxe, and plodding on, must make a calfe an oxe." Notice the spiked edges on those jam tins? Rather like, I think, the jagged cutting edge of Schopenhauer's intellect . . . Die Welt als Wille und Vorstellung. Here, in this room, is not only *my* mind but of course it is inevitable that the minds of others will be found within it – specially those of my children, my family. My mind is a vast cosmos, and in it the galaxies – interconnected – are all together in one magnificent symphonic whole – once again, part of Jung's philosophy. I refer you to Mantegazza's *Physiology of Love* – it has been said to be mere clever causerie but let us consider what we shall find in this room, of love!'

He moves toward my brother, who I notice actually flinches and shrinks a little from my father's outstretched hand:

'You are a brother – you are my dead brother's *namesake!*'

At this point my mother, gently whispering to him, pushes my little brother through the doorway to the hall and comes back to stand beside my sister and me, closing the door behind her. My father protests:

'No, don't send him off! It's important that a son should understand his father. To understand is to love. And his mother. It will not have escaped your notice that your mind is an integral part of the whole.'

He looks toward my mother again, whose hands are now round our shoulders.

'Need I draw your attention to the presence in here of a sister's mind too?'

We follow his eyes to the moustached photograph on the pile of books:

'The hirsute addition to my daughter's photograph? – *Roger!*

The lost baby who would have been now . . . ' He pauses and looks at my sister, 'almost twenty-two. The cylinders, you ask! – Blake's satanic mills – so-called civilisation – which connect of course – only I ran out of string – to my brother James. To his truncated life.'

My sister moves at last. Breaks away from my mother. She takes three steps forward to place her hand on my father's arm in a gesture of compassion. He pats her wrist:

'It can be argued that this construct is crude – there are bricks, a kettle and so on – I know that this is true, but what I'm trying to do here is to illustrate that what is occurring in the macrocosm also happens in the microcosm – in this room. I've done all this to try to help myself to understand all of the threads, all the memories – this is an attempt to bring them together, to give *final expression* to what for many years I have been struggling with.'

My agitation borders on nausea, but something in what my father is saying keeps me here. He continues:

'I've felt that I've merely been skating like a water-fly across the top of a pond of cognisance, whose depths, to my minuscule intelligence, I suspected, held more – *much* more. I finally realized that the key to that exotic-seeming mysterious abyss below, resides in the mundane, the leaden – the brickish, the kettlish, the ordinary things in life. Only by means of these, can I give ballast to my thoughts. Instead of them flying in all directions, here they are at last – entrapped like butterflies behind their collectors' paned boxes!'

He pauses. Walks quickly to the framed photo of my sister and reaching up taps its glass, smiling, eyebrows raised. Striding back to us, he says triumphantly:

'You see? Another connection! As I was saying, this is the first time, my darlings, that any man has caught, has sculpted his *own mind*!'

My father removes the shining torch from the chair that holds his dead brother's photo. Carefully, slowly, he turns it off. Then snuffs out the candles. I have to blink to accustom my eyes. I must watch my father vigilantly. The old feeling of panic has radiated through me and the tips of my fingers are tingling. He sits heavily on the now empty chair and spreads his arms wide:

'At last – I *know*! I'll be frank with you all. I've felt very much alone. For several years now I've felt no connection – this is an attempt to re-establish something . . . some means whereby . . . '

He breaks off and stands again. Starts his striding:

'I've been like a comet wandering in the outer reaches of an unpeopled universe. Blackness. Emptiness. There's been nothing. But I feel now I have come *streaming* back!'

My father's arm, lifted high, soars forward as he gesticulates:

'My light has come back into this room, has streamed back and now merges with yours – that of my family, my fellow man. I feel almost as a religious man might feel. That all knowledge is open to him! . . . All knowledge resides within him.'

He looks my way and closes his panegyric with the words:

'Jung, my dear – or perhaps I should say, my dear Jung – knows it all! Every man a universe. Not "I am in the *world*" – but "the world is in *me*!" How true that is. The *light!* At *last!*'

He runs to the window and the rings squeak on the rods as, with a flourish, he scoops back the curtains and sun fills the room. I lower my head, blinking at the incredible strength of the December light.

I'm afraid not of my father, no one could ever feel that, but rather for him – of what will become of him. In the last year, I've felt sorrow and grief that a comparative stranger has come to live in our house. To sleep for weeks. To walk at night. To talk like someone possessed. I want to wake up and find I'm back in Auchenflower. That he's reading under the blue jacaranda. And there are custard-apple trees and grasshoppers. And Acton when he played cricket with us on the flats and it was always sunny. And I feel pity too. But he doesn't need my solicitude. He's always said we're the ones who are out of step. Who don't understand. I watch him and I feel, more than ever today, the tenuousness of my father's spirits. My mother speaks at last:

'Norman dear, you've been in here for weeks now, in fact I

haven't seen you for two whole days. You haven't slept – or eaten or . . . '

'I won't talk to any doctor if that's what you're leading to. It's not *me* who requires help – look around at the world . . . '

My mother steps toward him:

'I think you need a rest – a nice, long *real* rest.'

I leave my parents talking, but before I go to my room I look back. What I see is more than a construct of my father's mind. I know now that he's explained its genesis, it's a plea for understanding.

I sit in the sun on the step at the back of the house. It'll be Christmas in ten days. But how different this year. My father won't be with us. I watch a wagtail hop delicately from a small twig of the fig tree to a branch higher up. The lower one quivers a little, then comes to rest. There's the sound of voices inside. I look at my watch. They're early, when I hoped they'd come late. Tried to will that they'd never come at all. I half-turn at the footsteps behind me and move over so the people have room beside me to step outside. My father speaks:

'And here, enjoying the sun, is my younger daughter who will perhaps one day communicate, via her canvases, with the world.'

I can't look at the two men who accompany him. I watch my father who stands with his back, his dear back, to the sun. And I see behind him the wagtail hop like lightning, to sit atop the empty bird-cage that still hangs from the fig tree – a stark reminder of the previous tenants. My father is finding words to tell me what I already know:

'These men, in their ignorance – perhaps their innocence – have come to transport me to parts hitherto unknown to me. I have been certified! But not, I'm afraid, as you would a precious and important letter whose pages hold between them a crucial message or the quintessential truth . . . '

One of the men shifts uncomfortably then takes my father's arm:

'Come along mate, you'll be right. As your good lady says – you need a break, a bit of a rest.'

And they're gone inside. I walk slowly down the ferny, unseasonably cold side of our house. Almost at its corner, I look across the front garden. I see my father put up clenched fists and playfully dance around on the grass, as if sparring. One of the men takes his hands, while the other opens the doors of the ambulance. They help him inside and one gives him the small case he's packed and offers him a cigarette, My mother is on the footpath. She waits, looking down the road for a few minutes after they've gone. I watch her return to the front door. Her progress is slow. She picks a daisy and looks down at it thoughtfully. Seeing her like this reminds me of pictures of people who pull the petals off a flower one by one saying:

'He loves me, he loves me not'

To do that would be so out of character for her. I wonder what she's thinking. She could be feeling sad about my father. She may be planning how she'll start dismantling the mind-model. Or debating whether she should touch it at all. Or she may just be pondering over whether she'll cook the corned beef for dinner, or the oxtail stew. With my mother, you never know because she doesn't talk about such things. She just does them. Perhaps she's walking slowly because she's so tired. I need to reveal myself. To go across from the side of the house where I'm hiding – so our paths would meet at the front step. Then I'd like to hug her and sit down there and talk with her and not have to hurry because she has to go. But I know I won't do that. I go back down the cool green path, the way I came.

We visit our father as often as we can. The hospital is far away. You have to take a bus to an outer northern suburb where the hills, as you approach them, turn gradually from blue to olive green and you can pick out faraway cottages in the folds and valleys. This forms a backdrop for the sprawling red brick building that houses my father.

On our fifth visit we bring a case of books he's asked for. Today he's no longer wearing the thick white coat that held his arms across his chest. And the room he's in hasn't got the same soft walls that gave a little when you leaned against them. He puts the case we brought under his bed, unopened. We only stay for an hour as we've left my little brother at home and my mother has to start work soon.

At the gate, my father hugs us each in turn. It's the very first time I've ever thought that his embrace is as much for him – perhaps more – as it is for me. His voice has a familiar emptiness, as he stands under the dark oak tree at the bus stop:

'I love you all . . . very much.'

He has foreseen the precipice he spoke of once before. And now he walks toward it. The attendant gently takes his arm. We wait till they're almost out of sight down the long pathway through the trees. A small change in the shape of his figure as he nears the distant red brick building, tells me that my father's turned to see that we're still here. Then he's gone.

24
'... BUT THEY WITHERED ALL WHEN MY FATHER DIED...'

I go to the dining room where the easel my father made stands at an angle beside the window. The old singlet I stretched and glued over some Masonite to make a canvas, is dry and ready for me to use. I look at the brushes and paints I got for Christmas, and touch a crumpled tube of Ebony Black. Then I open the drawer of the dresser where I keep my sketching things. There's the Dobell book from Sydney and the little packet of charcoal sticks. I take a sheet of drawing paper from those that are left in a small pile. A movement to my right makes me jump. A face appears at the window. It's Bernadette Shannon who always used to come round to the back when she visited. She looks so different now. I beckon to her. I hear the squeak of the hinges on the back flydoor. She comes into the room and stands behind me as I draw. She's chewing gum:

'Who's that?'
'Just a little boy.'
'I know – but *who?*'
'No one in particular.'

The child in my picture holds a bunch of new violets. I copy them from the bowl that stands nearby on the table. They're the first of the season. I grew them myself in a small round garden bed, deep in the shade among the ferns that flank the cool side path. I hear the gum moving rhythmically, moistly, between Bernadette Shannon's teeth. And there's the faint smell of peppermint. I take a rag from the ledge on the easel:

'You know how someone sits next to a window and light plays on one side of their head... and on one shoulder?'

I smudge the charcoal with the cloth, to give a soft shade to the contour of the forehead:

'Sometimes you can see the planes of the face through the hair that falls beside it.'